THE
LADY
OF
FIRE
AND
LIGHT

Book Cover by KD Ritchie at Story Wrappers Designs
Editing by Noah Sky and Jennifer Murgia
Illustrations by Etheric Designs
Map by Virginia Allyn

ISBN 979-8-9897885-4-5 (Paperback)
ISBN 979-8-9897885-3-8 (eBook)
ISBN 979-8-9897885-5-2 (Hardcover)

First Edition: August 2024
Snowshoe Press

BOOKS BY VICTORIA K. TAYLOR

THE FATE OF ASHES SERIES
A Crown of Star and Ash
The Lady of Fire and Light

To my sister,
For always being my other half

The Realm of
KRIGOR
Stars
Water
Earth
Fire
Mount Mors
NODARIA
The Celestial Throne
Atlas Keep
Arctos
Elmchon Woods
The Restless Channel
GANIEA
The Harvest Throne
The Mother Oak
Verdigris Marsh
Verta Fjor
Stonehall Castle
The Green Fortress
Lavalthon
The Red Citadel
WEXBRIDGE
Leybourne Hold
Ignisis
PRAITON
Terworth
MANIEL
The Ember Throne
Mevenia
Pentworth Harbor
Mount Cinis
LAENIMORE
The Sea Throne

N
W
E
S
Ironbalt Prison Camp
AUNECIA
Flykige
Fangdor Castle
Latchside Landing
THE EXILE CONTINENTS
HAVIA
Frostheim
BRIDAH
The Frost Throne
The Gray Gap
Light's Tower
ELBANIA
ZULON
Burningtide Sanctum
ORITUS
Durosi

THE LADY OF FIRE AND LIGHT

THE FATE OF ASHES PREQUEL NOVELLA

VICTORIA K. TAYLOR

CHAPTER 1

Blood matted her hair, staining the already red strands even darker as it dripped down. She flicked it out of her eyes as she strode through Light's Tower, her face covered in ash and soot, bleeding from various cuts and wounds—but still, she was smiling. Beaming.

"You look pleased." Aris fell into stride beside her, his handsome face a cool mask of neutrality. Only Val could see the shadow of a smile on his lips.

"You would be, too," she replied. "Especially if you had just enjoyed a lovely barbeque of Praiton soldiers. How could I not be in a good mood with the smell of burning flesh still in my nostrils?"

Aris let out a bark of laughter. "You Manielians truly are bloodthirsty wretches."

"And you Ganieans are pathetically passive," Val retorted, with a sickly-sweet grin, which he returned.

The Pillar Legion's general was clad in his usual gold armor—a relic from his time as a captain of the King's Guard in Ganiea. It was old and tarnished, with only hints of its former glory. She supposed some would say the same for its owner, but General Aris Calatos was far from being past his prime.

"Can you two stop flirting for once?" Katia appeared on Val's other side. The young female was also charred and bloodied, but her smile was as wide as her own.

"Trust me." Aris leaned past Val towards her smaller friend and smiled. "If I were flirting, Katia, you would know it."

Val rolled her eyes and shoved the philandering general aside, causing him to chuckle and Katia to flush.

"Can you please refrain from harassing my soldiers, *General*," Val demanded, putting on her best High Lady voice that had been drilled into her since birth.

Aris just winked at her, making her stomach flutter in the most obnoxious way.

The Pillar Legion was returning from battle and, for once, they were victorious. It had been a small skirmish—an interception of supplies from the coast of Zulon—but it had still been a long, bloody battle. Val was relieved that her regiment—led by her elite unit, the Fireflies—had not had any casualties. All of her soldiers were returning home; bleeding, bruised, and burnt, but otherwise alive.

Just then, a group of those soldiers staggered into the antechamber, carrying several large crates of supplies, which they dropped proudly at Aris's feet.

"Well done," the general remarked, shooting a look at Val. "I dare say this is enough weapons and herbs for the whole legion."

"*And*," Val said, grinning broadly, "we took out a very large squadron of Praitonian soldiers. Not to mention a few Manielian stragglers." She blew a singed piece of red hair out of her face, the smoldering scent making her nose twitch slightly.

Aris gave her his patented crooked smile—one that was always imbued with charm and confidence, yet never quite met those hazel eyes of his.

"This calls for a celebration," he announced. "Alert the kitchens! We have a feast to partake in."

The atrium of Light's Tower erupted into cheers and whistles, the smell of burnt flesh and singed clothing momentarily forgotten as the soldiers took the time to appreciate their victory. They all took off towards the dining hall, laughing and talking, filling the large, cavernous room with echoes of joy and merriment.

"Go get cleaned up," Aris said to Val, giving her arm a small squeeze. "You know where to find me if you want to have our own little celebration," he added in a whisper in her ear, giving her a lecherous wink that caused Val to gag and shove him off again.

"Honestly," Katia said, grabbing Val by the arm and ushering her away from the obnoxious general. "He truly has no shame."

"No," Val murmured distractedly. "He really doesn't."

This was Aris's way, though. And while the flirtations never amounted to anything—not with any of them within the Legion, at least—the healers and priestesses were another story. It seemed as if Aris's conquests were always tiptoeing down the stairs right when the rest of the Legion were waking for early morning training.

The other captains, Elric, Saros, and Lycas seemed to find this endlessly amusing. Val, however, always thought it to be in poor taste.

"He is the general, though," Katia added thoughtfully. They ascended the steps of the Tower towards the residential wing, the winding and twisting staircase an exhausting inconvenience after the day's events. "I suppose he can talk to us any way he wants."

"Are we talking about Aris?" Atria appeared out of nowhere, sprinting up the steps from behind and shoving in between them. The small, scrappy female shook back her short, pixie-length yellow and orange hair, smoke still unfurling from the burnt ends of her braids.

"Who else?" Katia huffed. "He tried to take Val to bed."

"He *always* tries to take Val to bed," another voice said, and Val flushed, opening her mouth to rebut this mortifying statement.

From behind them, Val's second, Lucia, stomped up the steps, cutting off her protests. Where Atria was petite and scruffy, Lucia was tall and willowy. Her features were much more feline than the others, accented with a shock of gorgeous, tawny hair. Between the four of them, Val's hair was the darkest, the reddest, the most pronounced red of all. A ruby amongst amber.

Lucia bumped in between Katia and Atria, pushing her way past all of them. She was the only one who wasn't covered in blood and soot, only sporting a few scratches and scuffs of dirt in places.

"He does *not* try to take me to bed," Val mumbled.

All three girls snorted at that.

"He definitely tries much harder for you than anyone else," Atria said with a snicker.

Katia hummed and Val shot her a warning look. "I mean, would it *really* be so bad?" Katia asked. "To bed him, I mean?"

Val and Atria both let out gags which caused Katia to look aghast. "*What?!* Atria, I know he's not your type" —Atria laughed at that. Her type was strictly more female than anything— "but Val, c'mon. You know he's attractive."

"Ugh, cut it out," Val moaned, giving an exaggerated shudder. "He is our general. Nothing more."

Though Lucia remained silent, Val knew she was secretly amused by it all. As one of the few Manielians who also came from a noble family, Lucia's mysterious, reserved nature only melted on the battlefield.

As the staircase leveled out, Lucia seized Val's arm and flicked a wrist at the other two, shooing them off.

"Get cleaned up," she commanded them, before she steered Val towards her room.

"What, are you going to bathe with me?" Val teased.

Lucia scoffed. "Wouldn't be the first time. How many creeks have we had to share after so many years in this blasted unit?"

"Too many."

Val's room was devoid of any personal touches—no trinkets on the desk, no decorations on the wall. The only sign this was actually her room were the many, many clothing items strewn about the small space. Armor, tunics, a few older, fancier dresses she never wore drowned all the furniture within the room.

"*Home*," she groaned and made to collapse, face-first on the bed, when Lucia's arm shot out and seized her around the middle.

"You are *filthy*," she reminded her. "I think there's still some brain matter on your shirt from the Praiton commander. Bath. *Now*."

Even though Val moaned in complaint, she knew Lucia was right. And when she dove, headfirst, into the deep, stone bathing pool it felt almost as good as the bed. Almost.

When she surfaced, it was to find Lucia sitting on the small stool by the pool, picking off her gloves and examining her chipped nails.

"Aren't you going to clean up?"

"Later," she said. "I did not get nearly as disgusting as you lot."

"That's what happens when I make you the rear guard," Val said, squeezing out a large dollop of soap into her grimy hair.

Lucia did not speak for a moment, picking dirt from her nails, until, "You blush every time Aris flirts with you, you know that, right?"

Val froze, her face heating.

Lucia pointed a chipped nail at her. "Yes, like that."

"I do *not!*" The mortification threatened to choke her. Did she *really* blush every time Aris joked around with her? Did he ever notice? The very thought made her want to plunge her head into the water and never resurface again.

"Oh, you definitely do," Lucia replied, smirking. "And I hope you know how much of a horrible idea it is for you to even consider—"

"I have *never* considered such a thing!" Val cried, half rising out of the pool before remembering she was naked and plunging back down. "How can you even think—"

"Because I know you hear the rumors, Val." Lucia's golden gaze cut through her protests. "The other captains, the soldiers . . . they do not like you. They do not like *us*."

Val sank further into the tub, the heat from her face beginning to trigger her Ember Magic, causing the pool to bubble slightly.

"Well, I know *that* already." She had not missed the whispering and the rumors. No one dared to say it to her face, but they all disparaged her. As the only female captain in the whole Legion, she expected backlash. But expected or not, it never failed to make her blood boil. With Maniel's alliance with Praiton and all its destruction, it was not uncommon for those aligned with the rebellion to hate Manielians just as much as Praitonians.

But to be female *and* Manielian nobility was a double sin in the Legion.

While most kingdoms allowed female fighters, it was not very common—especially in Maniel. Most went to temples to become priestesses, or else preferred a more docile approach to life. Val, on the other hand, preferred to fight. It was all she had ever known.

"Do not give them any reason to doubt you, Val," Lucia said softly. "You are a powerful warrior. The Fireflies are strong because of *you*. You deserve to be a captain." She rose from the stool. "And besides, Aris is a lout," she added, and left the room, leaving Val to chuckle to herself.

The feast was in full swing by the time Val descended from her room. It felt odd being clean after so many days locked in battle, living in her own filth and blood. She couldn't lie, it was amazing to have her hair feeling so soft and smelling like jasmine.

Lucia, Katia, and Atria were already seated in the dining hall, all with full plates of food and large mugs of ale. Val plopped down in front of them, scanning the hall for a familiar glint of gold, but Aris was nowhere to be seen. Feeling Lucia's gaze on her, Val averted her eyes, tucking into her own plate of steaming beef and potatoes.

Across the room, the other captains were holding court. Lycas—the only other Manielian captain—had a priestess sitting on his lap, tittering at something he had said. Val resisted the urge to roll her eyes. Lycas was her least favorite captain. As a Manielian commoner with little magic, he had somehow excelled as a fighter—mostly from getting into petty tavern brawls back home. Hardened and smarmy, Lycas was the leader in her ridicule and never missed an opportunity to put Val down in front of the other captains and soldiers.

Val knew if ever given the opportunity, she would roast him alive like a pig on a spit.

Katia noticed Lycas and the priestess as well and scoffed disapprovingly. "She should be chucked out of her temple for that," she muttered.

Val couldn't help but agree.

As the ale flowed, the soldiers got rowdier and rowdier. Even Katia and Atria were getting a little tipsy, banging their mugs on the table, joining the others in raucous songs from across Krigor. Lucia, however, sat calmly in her seat, nursing her mug of ale, watching the chaos with a sharp, golden eye.

Finally, Val finished her second mug of ale, feeling full and content— and a little woozy. The alcohol soothed her sore muscles, and quieted her spinning mind that wouldn't stop replaying the battle over and over again. That was the curse of a seasoned warrior. Every strike, every death, her mind parsed it over and over for ways to improve.

She had been forced to train in combat from a young age by her brothers. Her parents had hired a retired Master of Arms from the Red Citadel to train the older boys. While it wasn't expected for a daughter of a noble family to train, her eldest brother, Lorenzo, refused to be associated with the weak.

So Val trained, too.

After years of hard, brutal lessons which often left her bruised and beaten, she was now a master of the Manielian sword art. But all of that experience came at a cost.

Val stood from the long bench, and looked down at her unit. The Fireflies had been her lifeline since she had been cast out from Maniel. As the captain of the twenty-second regiment of the Pillar Legion, Val had not expected to form an elite unit. But the Fireflies had given her more than just a powerful extension of the rebellion . . . They had given her a family.

"I'm going to bed," she announced.

"Boo," Atria moaned, throwing a piece of potato at her, her eyes glazed and body swaying. "The night's still young, Val!"

"And *you* are very drunk," Val admonished, but she smiled at the small female, who seemed to have a hard time focusing on her. "And I am very tired. It has been a long few days."

Atria began to protest again, but Lucia stopped her with a stern, motherly look.

"Goodnight, Captain," Lucia said, giving her a small, rare smile.

Katia bid her another rather clumsy goodnight, and, with one last lazy wave over her shoulder at her sisters, Val left the dining hall. But instead of heading for the stairs towards the residential wing, she headed back to the kitchen and piled a plate full of hot food fresh from the pots over the fire.

When she hadn't seen Aris in the dining hall, she already knew where she would find him. Sure enough, as she walked down the darkened hallway of offices and studies on the lower floor, she saw the flicker of torchlight coming from the general's quarters. She knocked, waited for his call to enter, and pushed open the door.

Aris was sitting behind his desk, maps spread across the surface, a surprisingly worn look on his face. He had removed the gold armor, and was dressed in a plain, white cotton tunic that made him look more casual than she had ever seen him.

"Valeria," he said, looking up and giving her that same, vaguely friendly smile, the tiredness she had noted gone in an instant. "To what do I owe the pleasure? Did you decide to take me up on my offer to have a more *intimate* celebration?"

Val narrowed her eyes at him. "Very funny." She stepped fully into the room, and placed the plate down on the one empty bit of desk she could find. "I just wanted to bring you this."

Aris's eyebrow rose at the plate, and a small, crooked grin crossed his face.

"Thank you, Valeria," he murmured.

It was rare to see the general alone, and Val did not fancy leaving quite so soon. Removed from an audience for him to perform to, she found Aris to be strangely subdued. As if his true self was within reach for the first time.

She moved into the room, sitting down in the high-back chair across from him. "You did not want to join the feast that you so benevolently called for?"

Aris let out a tired sigh, rubbing at the back of his neck. "Unfortunately, I had some work to attend to first. I thank you for the food, though. I was rather hungry."

"What work possibly takes precedence over our victory today, General?"

Aris moved a piece of paper free of the map he had been pouring over and pointed towards a spot on the eastern side of the continent. Val leaned forward and looked up at him, her brow furrowed.

"Bridah," she said.

Aris nodded. "Bridah."

"And what is it about Bridah that troubles you, General?" she inquired. "Out of all the kingdoms, it is the most insulated. Surely, it is the least of our worries."

"This is true, it's protected by its fjords," he agreed. "However, what kingdom borders Bridah?"

She knew already, but still, her eyes moved inadvertently to Bridah's neighboring kingdom.

Maniel.

Aris saw it in her face. "Now, tell me. What is the one thing that can thwart ice?"

Looking up at him slowly, the answer they both knew remained unspoken. "They can't," she breathed. "They have tried multiple times. The fjords stop them, and if they don't, we do."

Aris did not respond. His finger traced the shape of Maniel on the map, his gaze lingering on it. "This is true," he said again. "But still . . . I worry they will conquer the fjords. And if they do that, we may not stand a chance."

Val did not speak. She knew the Manielian army well—had trained with them, even fought with them in the times before the war. Titus had ensured the strongest fighters, both magically and physically, were heading his army.

"Titus is the strongest Ember Magic user in almost a millennium," Aris said. "If there was somebody who could melt the entire fjord surrounding Frostheim, it's him."

Val knew this was true. She had seen Titus do awful yet incredible things in her long life. She also knew his son, Lynos, to be of the same, horrible power. The thought of Lynos made something run cold inside of her, and she fought a small shiver.

"What are you thinking of doing, then?" she asked. "What precautions?"

Aris sighed, the cool, confident ease slipping again, showing her just the tiniest hint of exhaustion behind those hazel eyes. "Possibly setting up a post within Bridah to guard against any potential Manielian invasions. I have a contact within Bridah who may be willing to help us find someplace."

Val studied Aris carefully, taking in the bags under his eyes, the shadows on his defined jaw. As the founder of the Pillar Legion, Aris had every right to be considered the Knight Commander, but he had insisted on only being a general. Val had always wondered why. Aris was charming and cocksure, never one for modesty or humility, and yet he insisted on staying at a lower rank than he deserved.

"You know, we can help you with this," she told him softly. "You don't have to bear it alone." She leaned over the desk towards him and gave him a gentle, teasing smile. "That is why you have captains, General."

Aris smiled, his gaze roving her face curiously, leisurely. She never knew what it was about Aris's lingering glances—how they made her feel exposed, as if he were devouring her slowly. Even though everything told her to look away, she didn't.

"Are you offering?" he asked, his eyes still doing their slow, casual feast of her.

"I am always at your service, General."

A lazy, cocky grin spread across Aris's face. "I will definitely remember that."

And just like that, the spell was broken. She rolled her eyes, and Aris laughed.

Val got to her feet and made towards the door, pausing to look back at Aris one more time.

"Eat," she reminded him. "We cannot defeat Maniel in a night, and neither can you."

Aris chuckled as he refocused on her again. "Thank you, Valeria," he murmured.

Val nodded and turned to go, feeling her heart beat fiercely in her chest, and no doubt making her turn a bright, ridiculous red.

CHAPTER
2

The next morning, Val wanted nothing more than to have the day off. Her body ached from fighting and sleeping on the hard forest floor, and her bed felt *so* warm and comfortable. Instead, she was midway through a dream when her door crashed open and Lucia strode in.

"Lucia, for the love of the Mother—" Val cried, sitting upright in bed, an explosion of smoke and spark shooting out of her involuntarily.

Lucia stamped out the covers that had caught flame with an expressionless face, and jerked back the sheets.

"You're late for training," she said. "That is no way for a captain to behave."

Val let out a tiny groan as Lucia flapped her sheets against her impatiently. Lucia was always stern and a little commandeering, but she had never ripped Val out of bed with such force before. And as Val blinked the sleep out of her eyes and peered up at her friend, it was to see the furrow of her brow and the set of her shoulders. Val knew that look—had seen it before when someone whispered something derogatory about her to one of the Fireflies. Judging by the hard set to Lucia's jaw, it was clear the naysayers must have grown in strength and volume since she had been away.

With a twisting feeling in her gut, Val rose from the bed. And although every muscle in her body protested, she ignored it as she dragged herself towards her wardrobe.

She knew Lucia was right—knew that her insistence that Val put on a show of strength at all times was the only way to silence the vitriol buzzing around Light's Towers like a swarm of angry hornets. But she could not deny that she *hated* having to yield to it.

When she and Lucia finally arrived at Light's Tower's training arena in the back courtyard, it was to find the Laenimorian captain Elric, and Lycas already training their own units. Water and fire flashed within the ring and Val resisted the urge to smirk at the weak, pathetic sparks Lycas sent from the end of his tarnished sword.

They both looked up as Val arrived, clad in her brown leather armor with her hair tied back in a braided ponytail. Elric merely scoffed when he saw her. The Sea Fae did not like her, that much was obvious, but he was never outright vindictive to her. Not like Lycas.

"Good of you to join us, *Lady Augusta*," the runt sneered at her as she passed. Val let out a low growl and made towards him, but Lucia caught her around the middle, jerking her subtly back to her side.

"Ignore him," she hissed out of the corner of her mouth. "After all, what's a sheep to a lion, Val?" Val bit her tongue, seething, but knew she was right. She had plenty of practice ignoring Lycas's snide remarks. But still . . . the thought of lighting him up like a piece of kindling made her smile inside, just a little. With that image firmly in her mind, it was easier.

Already, Val's unit was in the large circular training ring towards the far end of the clearing. The small, rounded enclosure was shaded by the cliffs surrounding them, filtering in a light breeze that whipped through Val's hair as she approached her two senior officers. While Katia and Atria had not been traditionally trained in swordplay, like she had, Val had personally honed each of the Fireflies' skills for the last several years. She felt a spark of pride as she watched her two sergeants spar, their movements like a dance, mirroring the other with impeccable precision.

Both girls stopped and looked up as Lucia and Val arrived, Atria glaring at Lycas, crackling with anger.

"Don't bother," Val told her, holding her head high as she drew her golden dual swords from their sheaths. They twinkled in the light, the etchings of her family's legacy illuminated in the early morning sun. A reminder every time she fought of what she had lost. Of what she fought to destroy. To erase.

Val and Lucia squared off within the ring, both holding their swords out towards each other—a custom in Manielian dueling before beginning to spar, their swords coming together in bursts of spark and flame.

Since she was a child, Val had been taught to feel the blades as an extension of herself, an aspect of the Manielian swordplay that was drilled into each of them at birth. And although it was something she had worked endlessly to perfect, as each blade slashed and scissored in perfect synchronicity, today she felt disconnected from her whole body. Her muscles and bones ached with each movement; the fatigue of the battle still fresh in every sinew.

Meanwhile, Lucia's magic was strong and steady—almost annoyingly so. Ember Magic was tied so tightly to her feelings—to her own personal emotional state. The exhaustion from the days before meant that, today, Val's bursts of fire were sputtering and flickering like a waning candle, barely able to keep up with Lucia's stable, unwavering flame.

"You are not concentrating," Lucia hissed as her double blades spun around her, her flames expanding out in a ferocious wave, causing Val to curse and leap back. "Channel your magic, Captain. Focus."

Val grit her teeth, attempting to imbue as much of her fury into the flames licking her own golden swords as she could. They blew up, shooting into the air like an inferno, causing Lucia to smirk.

"That's more like it," she murmured, and then lunged for her again.

Val and Lucia battled across the arena, Lucia's orange flames and Val's bright white ones dueling and flickering. As the two Manielian females scorched the dirt of the training ring around them with sheer heat, Val could feel the scrutinizing glares of Elric, Lycas, and their units, but she didn't let it faze her. Not this time.

Sparks shot from her golden blades—which were burning, white-hot—as steam began to rise from her ankles. She whirled and danced with her second in command, grinning as she met each of Lucia's flaming blades with her own. Lucia's family magic was strong, but not as strong as the Augusta's. Her white flames were billowing with it, overwhelming her blades with heat and light.

Val breathed out a hot gust of air, then, with a swirling slash, she sent both Lucia's blades flying. They spun in the air before landing, points down, with a sizzling thud in the ground in front of her.

Lucia stood, stunned for a second. She could sense Katia, Atria, Lycas, Elric, and their collective units all watch as the swords fell. And then the Fireflies and the rest of Val's regiment were erupting into whoops, catcalls, and whistles. A wide grin spread over Lucia's face as she gave her captain an appreciative nod, while Katia and Atria flocked to her, thumping her hard on the shoulder. Val was enveloped by the cheers and laughter of her unit until a snide, sneering voice cut through the din.

"What in the Mother was that?"

Val's smile and those of her unit's faded as Lycas approached, an evil, mocking glint in his brown eyes.

"Are you supposed to be a captain or a circus performer, *Lady Augusta?*"

Val sensed her unit stiffen. Atria was crackling with anger, but Val laid a hand on her hot wrist.

"If I am a *circus performer* what does that make you, Lycas?" Val sneered. "A clown?"

Katia sniggered beside her, but Lycas just gave her a hateful, jeering look. "Very funny, *my Lady*. Does your *husband* find that funny?"

All the air seemed to seep out of the training ring, and a warm, melting feeling began to trickle down Val's chest. Her unit all turned to look at her—Atria and Katia's stunned faces were confused, questioning. Lucia, however, remained stoic.

"I do not have a husband," Val snapped quickly, but her voice wavered as her lungs constricted. The training ring shrunk around her, the edges of her vision going fuzzy. In the end, she knew it was useless, knew that nothing short of killing Lycas would shut him up now.

The little runt moved closer to her, that pale, freckled face leering as he drawled, "*Really?* Is that so? I got some interesting information the other day from one of our spies still in the Ember Court. Do they know? Does your precious unit know that you were betrothed to none other than Prince Lynos of the Ember Throne?"

Blood pounded in Val's ears. She could feel the weight of everyone's stare on her, could feel her breath coming in short gasps as Lycas moved closer to her, his sneer growing wider.

"So, who is the clown now, *my Lady?* Did your parents sell you to him? Like some trussed up concubine? Every circus needs a *whore* to put on display," he snarled.

It happened all at once. Val barely had time to blink at the insult, before all around her, the Fireflies had their swords drawn and were advancing towards Lycas like rabid dogs. Lycas let out a terrified yell, drawing his own sword just in time to deflect that of Lucia's, Katia's, and Atria's, who advanced on the squealing captain with murderous rage in their eyes.

The force of their collective blow knocked his weapon flying, and all three of Val's most trusted soldiers held their swords against the captain's throat. Lucia stood at the helm, her golden eyes flashing with such hatred and disgust that she was amazed Lycas wasn't reduced to ash where he trembled.

"No, Lucia! Katia, Atria! Wait!" Val cried, moving forward her hands outstretched, but she froze as Lucia jabbed her sword towards the quivering captain's throat.

"Apologize," Lucia growled, her sword pressing into the soft flesh of his jugular, causing Lycas to whimper. From the edge of the arena, Elric and his unit were converging on them, swords drawn.

Flames were beginning to creep down Lucia's blade as she shoved the steel even harder into Lycas's throat.

"Apologize!" she shouted again.

"Lucia!" Val rushed to put herself between her unit and the cowering captain, but it was as if her commanding officers did not hear her.

"Get them off me!" Lycas was shrieking from the floor. *"Elric!* Elric, get the general! Get these vicious harpies off—"

But Val silenced him with an explosion of white-hot flames. The wall of fire erupted from her, rippling across the arena, so hot and vicious that even the fire resistance all Manielians had was overwhelmed as Lucia, Katia, Atria, and Lycas all let out a yell of pain and sprang apart.

"*Enough!*" Val roared over her flames. Her body hummed with anger, but the small twinge of panic caused her fire to billow to tantamount heights, threatening to overwhelm the entire arena. It knocked all three of her commanding officers to the ground, the flames rippling from her like a blazing fence as she stood between her furious unit and Lycas. With a breath, she extinguished them.

Lycas got up, trembling, covered in dirt and soot and spitting in fury. Shoulders shaking with barely suppressed rage, Elric hurried to his side.

"Fiend!" Elric shouted at her, his eyes wide. "You cannot even control your own soldiers! You are not fit to be a captain!"

Val, who turned to help her fallen officers up off the ground, bristled at this.

"Shut up!" Atria yelled from behind Val. "Captain Augusta is a stronger fighter than either one of you, and you just hate—"

But the captain whirled and suddenly struck the small female so hard that she went flying to the ground again. Val moved in a blink of an eye. Fire claimed her vision, a burning, flickering, *fury* that made her draw both of her blades and move straight for the captain. Her swords scissored in midair . . . only to crash down onto a large, gold broadsword.

Aris stood between her and the Sea Fae captain, the large weapon glittering in the low afternoon sun, his peridot eyes blazing as he looked at her over the locked blades.

"*Get out of my way,*" she growled.

Aris did not move an inch as she pushed furiously down on his blade, fire beginning to roar from the hilt of her sword.

"*Valeria!*" he yelled. "*Stop!* Stand down this instant!"

Val snarled, her gaze still locked onto Elric over Aris's gold armored shoulder.

"*Valeria!*"

Finally, Val's eyes moved from the quivering Laenimorian captain to the golden green irises of the Pillar Legion's general. Their gazes locked. Val felt the fire extinguish in her and her sword dropped. She stepped back.

Aris lowered his own sword slowly, still eyeing her with a look of leery disappointment. He leaned past her and offered his hand to Atria.

"Are you okay?"

Atria nodded, her cheek a bright red from where Elric had hit her. The mark made the fire start bubbling inside of her again.

"Valeria, my office *now*," Aris said through gritted teeth, and for once, his tone was not cool and collected. Head bowed, Val sheathed her swords. Aris turned to Elric, and this time there was no questioning the rage in his expression.

"I will deal with *you* later," he snarled, and then, grabbing Val by the elbow, he marched her back towards Light's Tower.

They took the long walk to Aris's office in a tense silence. Val was still breathing hard, waves of her Ember Magic steaming off her body. Her heart pounded in her ears, angry staccato rhythms that echoed with their footsteps in the empty corridor of Light's Tower's commanding offices.

Aris opened the door to his office for her, still not looking her in the face. Val marched in and threw herself into the same chair she had vacated the night before; arms crossed, face set. Aris shut the door with a gentle snap and walked briskly back to his desk and sank into his chair.

They sat there, rigid in their chairs, anger filling the space between them. Val was nearly vibrating with fury, Lycas's words still echoing in her ears.

Did your parents sell you to him like some trussed up concubine?

A chill of rage wrapped itself around the flame in her chest and her throat burned with unshed tears of embarrassment. Lycas had well and truly hit a nerve.

Finally, she heard Aris draw in a deep, steadying breath.

"What were you thinking, Valeria?"

Val huffed but did not answer. She was too angry to think straight— to even *see* straight. Aris was a golden blur in her vision as he rose from behind the desk and walked around it to stand in front of her, forcing her to have to stare at his boots. She refused to look up.

"Valeria," he said again. When she didn't answer, his hand reached out and grasped her chin, jerking her gaze up to his. Val's breath caught. For a second, they just looked at each other, his fingers still firmly on her jaw. As she looked into those hazel eyes, something in her seemed to sizzle.

She took a deep breath. The flames inside her began to dim, her blood pressure simmering down. Aris seemed to note this, and his fingers relaxed on her as she released a steaming breath that she had been holding. Her body finally cooled.

"Better?" he asked. She realized she was still gazing up at him, his fingers now softly holding her steady, before she coughed and looked away, nodding.

Aris released her and moved back to his desk, sitting down, and studying her quietly. The anger that was in his eyes back at the training arena was gone, replaced now with only concern.

"I know it is unfair of me to ask this of you," Aris said after a moment, "but I feel I must. Some say I took a risk appointing you as a captain."

Val stiffened, her heart giving a feeble tremble at this.

"But I do not regret it," Aris continued. "Not for a second. You are one of the strongest magic wielders we have in the Legion, Valeria. After our last battle against Maniel on our shores, there was no question in my mind that you deserve this position."

Val looked up at him, an image of the battle he mentioned flashing through her mind. It had been the scariest day of her life . . . The day a small battalion from her wretched kingdom had found her new home five years ago. How they had attempted to destroy it . . . burn it. Taking in a deep breath, she fought back the memory of Light's Tower in flames. And even though her chest ached at the thought, she would not let the tears fall. She could not. She *was* a captain, after all.

"Thank you," she whispered finally.

Aris gave her a small smile. "I know the others give you a hard time," he said. "And trust me, Elric and Lycas *will* be dealt with. But I have to ask you this favor, Valeria. Please try to comport yourself as a captain should. Do not stoop to their level. If not for my sake, then for your own."

"They do not respect me," Val said finally. It came out in a whisper, pained, and choked. "I do not know how I can act like a captain if they will not allow me to do so."

"Your unit does not believe that," he said. "If today was anything to go by, you have earned their utmost respect and loyalty. And that is what matters."

Val bit her lip, staring down at the floor. Her eyes stung with unshed tears as she thought about her soldiers . . . her sisters. Aris was right. She knew they would protect her until the bitter end. And while the thought warmed her heart, it was far from a comforting one.

She looked up at the general. "I am sorry for my officers' reactions today. I did not think that they would—"

"Defend you?" Aris smirked. "Those girls would die for you, Valeria. You should have known that. However, . . ." He paused, his brow furrowing slightly, looking troubled. "As general, I cannot allow soldiers attacking a Legion captain to go unanswered. I will have to discipline them."

Val had expected this, had been braced for it. In Maniel, insubordination on that level warranted an extreme punishment. Flogging, beating, imprisonment . . . The thought of Lucia, Atria, and Katia being punished in that way just for defending her . . .

Aris saw the fear in her eyes, and he gave her a gentle smile. "Don't worry," he assured her. "I am chalking this situation up to mutual combatants, so they will most likely get clean up duty and maybe extra laps at training. There will be no corporal punishment for them."

Val let out a relieved sigh, but felt a squirm of anxiety needle through her. "But won't Lycas and Elric be angry at your decision?"

Aris snorted. "Let them. I am their general. If they have a problem with it, I would like to see them try and challenge it."

Val gave a dry laugh. "I promise you, General, it will be *me* they try to challenge, not you."

Aris studied her. Gods, he *always* seemed to be studying her. At least this kind of long, scrutinizing stare wasn't nearly as discomforting as his all-consuming, lingering gazes that never failed to make her heart race like some mad horse.

"Well, we will see to that," he said finally. "And besides, while I have you here, there is something I would like to discuss with you."

"Oh?" Val's heart did the weird, annoying flutter it always did around the general. She wanted to rip it out and throw it across the room out of pure spite.

"I am attempting to do a full reconnaissance on the High King of Maniel and his family," Aris said, much to Val's shock. "I think the Peruro family are our biggest worries when it comes to Bridah's safety."

"I agree," Val said quietly.

"And since you so kindly offered your assistance to me last night," Aris added with a sultry, knowing grin that made her face flush and her eyes roll simultaneously, "I thought you might be the best person to work with on this."

Val glanced up at him, her long curtain of hair falling into her face. "Is that the only reason you think I'd be the best person for this?" she found herself asking in a soft voice. "Or for another reason?"

Aris hesitated. That piercing, searching look appeared in his eyes again as they seemed to sweep every inch of her face. When he didn't respond for a beat too long, Val knew.

"You overheard."

He bowed his head. "Lycas's voice may have . . . carried a bit."

Val let out an indignant huff, her arms tightening over her chest. "Of course it did. He wanted you to hear it. Wanted everyone to hear."

Aris's gaze was still hard and firm, but a flicker of sympathy glimmered in those hazel eyes.

"Why did you not tell us?"

Val scoffed. "It's not exactly something you'd want to advertise, is it? They hate me enough already for being Manielian nobility. But to be *betrothed* to—" Val broke off, a chill running down her spine at the memory of the High Prince of Maniel. How wicked the spark was in his red eyes when they had run down her body. How they had looked at her as if she were an offering on an altar.

She shifted in her seat and lifted her chin higher, attempting to regain control of her now pounding heart as Aris watched her closely. "The prince was and still is a bloodthirsty brute. I had no choice in the arrangement, but I am ashamed even so."

"I thought the Peruro's were your cousins?" Aris inquired.

Val looked away, her face flushing. "They are. Intermarriage within powerful bloodlines is common within noble families. The older the family, the stronger the magic is. So the families tend to marry each other to strengthen it even more."

Aris nodded, his face still neutral, placid. "Yes, this happens in Ganiea as well," he murmured thoughtfully.

"My parents thought it would be the most advantageous match," Val scoffed. "I was inordinately powerful for a female in my line, though you wouldn't know it by how my brothers treated me. But because of this, I was something of a hot commodity."

Her resentment reverberated through every syllable, remembering how her parents had attempted to trade her like chattel. She had been paraded from lord to lord, from noble family to noble family like a prized chicken. When they had finally settled on the most prestigious family they could find, it had been a negotiation. The Peruro family had bestowed their son's hand to the Augusta's as if it were some holy blessing from Calida Herself. And even then, their betrothal came with conditions.

Val could not be seen in armor or with weapons. As the princess of the Ember Throne, she had to be a lady. While the Manielians prided themselves on being ferocious warmongers, the traditional role of the Princess of the Ember Throne was to be just that. A princess.

Val was *not* a princess.

"What happened to the wedding?" Aris asked.

Val's arms tightened across her chest. "It never happened. One of the conditions for my hand was that my brothers were to join the king's most elite, deadly unit." Val fought a shiver at the thought of the Blood Riders. The small unit was responsible for more than half the deaths in the war alone. "Of course, they joined gladly. That was when Maniel began their conquests at Praiton's side. When I did not agree with my family's stance, my brothers made me choose. Join them—join *Praiton*—or be banished from the family and Maniel forever." The thought of her brothers made cold fear prick her chest. Before the image of her middle brother, Leo, could overwhelm her, she shook him from her mind.

He cannot touch you here.

She looked up at Aris and she saw understanding in those hazel eyes, the colors so like that of a peridot stone. Always seeming to say so much while not revealing anything at all.

"You chose banishment," he finished for her.

She nodded. "I did."

She had lost her family, her home, her name. Every time Lycas called her Lady Augusta it sent an agonizing flame of pain through her core. She had discarded that name and all that it came with.

"I remember the day you came here," Aris mused. "You were bruised, beaten. Barely alive."

Val closed her eyes, mostly so she did not have to look at the general across from her. She didn't think she could stand to see his sympathy. She breathed deeply, the burning pain she felt in her chest intensifying as she fought for words.

It had been twenty years since she had come here. Since Nodaria had fallen. Since she been forced to choose. She could still feel the burns on her face, the ache in her body as her brothers held her down and . . . Val swallowed.

"My older brothers attempted to beat me into submission," she whispered after a long while. "Lorenzo and Leonidus were staunch supporters of the war. And they made it their mission to make sure I was, as well. By force."

Her brothers had beaten her within an inch of her life. Both extraordinarily strong Ember Magic wielders, they took turns beating and burning her, attempting to sway her position on the war. Leo, the younger brother, was more bloodthirsty than Lorenzo. He did most of the damage. And when she was one more hit from death, her oldest brother stepped in. Lorenzo had taken pity on her, given her a choice: yield or be banished. She had made her decision.

When she recounted this to Aris, she saw his eyes close, his long, calloused fingers rubbing his chin.

"I'm so sorry, Valeria," he murmured finally.

The feeling of Leo's hot hands on her made a cold shiver roll up her spine. Tears and panic overtook her before Val shook her head vehemently, pushing it all back. "They can say what they want about me," she said. "But I have sacrificed for this cause. I am steadfast in my mission to you, General."

Aris looked at her for a long moment, before the corner of his mouth lifted slightly in that same, heart-racing smile. "I do not have a single doubt about that," he said. "So, will you join me? Will you help me in learning more about the nobility of Maniel?"

Val did not hesitate. "I will tell you everything I know."

CHAPTER 3

Val and Aris began their reconnaissance mission on Maniel the next day and continued for several days. After dinner, when everyone had retired to their rooms for the night, Val would go straight to Aris's office and tell him everything she knew about the Manielian noble families. And, most importantly, what she knew about the High King of the Ember Throne.

True to his word, Aris did not give Lucia, Atria, or Katia severe punishments. They were relegated to nightly clean up duty for a month, as well as an extra five miles added to their run every day. While some would think that this punishment was fair, the snide whispers that followed Val down the hall like acrid smoke indicated Lycas and Elric, did not.

The discord spread by the captains was growing more and more palpable within Light's Tower. Even the foot soldiers began to sneer at her as she passed. She knew the cat was out of the bag about her betrothal . . . And all of Light's Tower knew.

Still, as the days went by, Lucia, Atria, and Katia had not once mentioned anything about Lycas's accusation. She knew it was because they did not know how to ask her about it. None of them would've had even the slightest clue about what her family had planned for her. None, except for Lucia, who came from the Niro family, a lesser noble family, but a noble family all the same. She had known all along, but it was never something they explicitly spoke about.

Val sighed and shifted in her usual chair in Aris's office. It was late. The candlelight pouring over the many pieces of parchment and books on genealogy sprawled out in front of them caused the shadows to flicker over the pages, making the tiny ornate words harder to read than usual.

Val had spent the last couple nights telling Aris everything she had ever heard about the Peruro magic. Different families had different specialties—this was true all across Krigor. The Augusta family had the ability to produce white-hot flames, whereas the family that the evil Praiton Chief, Decius, hailed from had strong blue fire.

The Peruros, however, were an exceptional case. Descended directly from the goddess Calida's first son, the Peruros were often referred to as Born of the Dragon. Their resilience to intense heat surpassed any other Manielian family's, but the Peruros guarded the true extent of their magic most jealously. Val knew little of these secrets, having never been close enough to the royal family to hear anything other than rumors. She could only tell Aris things she had observed, theories she had heard. The rest, they had to find through their own research.

"I don't think I can read another sentence," Val groaned, her eyes drooping as they struggled to take in even one more word. The image of High King Atticus—Titus's grandfather—and his golden glaive swam in her vision as she yawned widely.

Aris was quietly perusing the pages, his brow furrowed, his long fingers curled under his chin. The only sign that he was even a little bit as exhausted as she was were the occasional yawns that would slip out of his mouth, which he quickly tried to stifle with a fist.

"Well, at least we have lots of information on Titus's grandfather." His voice was hoarse from the hours of silence they had been sharing. "Not much to be said about their Ember Magic, though."

"Manielians tend to be very secretive about our abilities," Val replied, yawning widely. "It gives us an edge in battle, you see."

"I definitely do see." With a sigh, he closed the book with a loud thump. Dust exploded into the air as the pages slammed together, causing Aris to cough slightly. "Well, there is only so much we can do in one night."

Val let out a small grunt in reply, laying her head down on Aris's desk and resting her weary eyes. Spending hours reading about all the families she hated really took it out of her.

Aris chuckled, and she heard him stand. "It sounds like we need a little pick me up," he said. A large mug of very strong-smelling ale was placed in front of her. Val let out a moan of longing, and reached for it like a desperate animal.

Aris poured himself one and came around the desk to sit in the spare chair beside hers. "Cheers," he said, giving her a gentle, tired smile.

She smiled back. "Cheers." Their mugs clinked, and they both took a long pull from it and simultaneously sighed.

"Thank you again for this," Aris said, his finger circling the rim of his cup. "You have been a big help."

"I'm honestly surprised you asked," she said. "You hardly ever ask for help, *General.*" The emphasis on the word made him chuckle again, that same lazy, self-assured noise that made her toes curl in the strangest way.

"Well, forgive me, I sometimes forget I have those like you."

"You always do things alone," Val hedged, not looking up from her mug. She did not know how forthcoming Aris was. He was almost always a closed book—a pretty face and a flirty smile laid over an image of a general who was always in charge, always in control. Even now, the flicker of an expression passed over his face, overshadowing that lazy, arrogant smile.

"Force of habit, I suppose." He took a swig of his drink, as if for a distraction.

It seemed as if Aris was nothing but a series of distractions. She always watched him, noted how those smiles of his never quite reached his eyes as he flirted.

Val desperately wanted to know what made the enigmatic general tick. She knew that he had been cast out by the Prince of Ganiea in an attempt to save his life after the Harvest Throne fell to Praiton. Knew that it had destroyed him to see Ganiea's High King fall, as head of the King's Guard—not to mention leaving someone he considered a brother in Praiton's hands. This had all created the male before her, and the curious way he led the Pillar Legion.

Val had lots of experience with armies and militaries in Maniel. The Knight Commander of these forces *never* got their hands dirty. They sat in the rear, commanded from afar. Aris was not like that. Not only did he refuse to even be *called* the Knight Commander—even though as founder of the Pillar Legion, he technically *was*—he was always in the thick of every battle. Every maneuver or training, he was right there with the rest of them.

"Were you used to handling everything alone as a knight in

Ganiea?" she asked.

Aris did not answer. His finger still swirled around the rim of the cup, his eyes following the movement. "I mostly guarded the royal family. I was assigned to Prince Minos mostly," he said finally. "We'd known each other since we were children. He was my best friend."

Val watched him. He didn't look up at her.

"Have you heard any news from Ganiea? How is Minos faring?"

A twitch in his jaw. A small fracture in the mask. "I have heard nothing but what our spies have told us."

"And?" Val was pushing, she knew she was, but she always felt like Aris needed to be pushed. That perfect mask of his always shone so brightly, and the need to see behind it was too strong for her.

"He is alive," he replied stiffly. "Complying."

"General—" Val began, but Aris turned to her and smiled. It was like watching a shadow move away from the moon. It lit up his handsome face, but those eyes . . . those eyes remained empty.

"It's late," he said, placing his mug down on the desk. "We should turn in. Unless . . ." He leaned towards her, his now free hand reaching to brace on the back of her chair, that same sultry grin spreading across his face. "You wish to turn in together."

Val's eyes narrowed. She knew what he wanted, knew he was waiting for her to let out a groan of disgust and dismiss him. The flirting, the arrogance, it was all a front. She saw this now.

So, she called him on it.

She moved closer to him, their knees now touching. The surprise that crossed Aris's face as she leaned forward and brushed his thigh lightly with her finger only confirmed her suspicions.

"Maybe we should," she whispered, looking up at him from

underneath her eyelashes. They were so close she knew he could feel the heat radiating from her—the only tell that she was nervous. Her hand rested heavily on his leg, his thigh solid with muscle. His eyes fell on her hand, then darted back up to look her in the eyes. Her heart beat so loud she could feel it in her ears.

And then he looked away. Clearing his throat, he got to his feet and moved back behind the desk. She let out a long-held breath that shook slightly.

"It's late," Aris said again, still not looking at her. Val watched him fidget, moving about the room gathering the papers and the books, almost as if needing his hands to be doing something. Then she let out a small laugh and rose to her feet.

"I thought so," she said softly. Val stood, watching as Aris stacked the books, still not looking up at her. A spark of frustration flared in her and, without thinking, Val reached forward and slammed her hand down right on top of the book the general was attempting to gather up. The force of her palm against the cover caused a swell of steam to escape from underneath her hand, sparks flying. Aris jumped and looked up at her in alarm. Their eyes locked.

"I see through you, General."

And then she turned on her heel and walked out the door.

"Are you okay, Captain?" Katia peered at her anxiously over their breakfast the next morning. Val's three officers were practically falling asleep onto their eggs. Between their late-night punishments and their early morning runs, all three of them looked gaunt and weary. Lucia's hair was ever so slightly disheveled and Katia was sagging into Atria, her eyelids drooping.

Val was not feeling so chipper herself. Last night in Aris's office had set her on edge. She wondered if he was going to invite her back tonight after what happened. The thought of his leg under her hand still made her fingertips tingle. The brief second that she'd made him vulnerable . . . Unmasked. The look on his face then still played endlessly in her mind.

She took a sip of her coffee. "I'm fine," she replied with a terse smile.

Katia did not look convinced but was stopped from prying more by Atria laying her head down on the table with a *thump*.

"I cannot believe how long we have to do clean up duty for," she moaned.

"We could have been imprisoned or flogged, like in Maniel," Lucia said, cutting a piece of sausage with prim movements. "Careful what you complain about, Atria."

Atria's mouth snapped shut and she hastily looked back down at her plate.

"Still, the general could have punished those captains, too," Katia mumbled. "They were the ones who started the trouble."

"No one forced you lot to attack Lycas." Val pushed a grilled tomato around her plate, but her heart swelled with affection at the memory. "Although I am grateful to you all for it."

"It was worth it," Atria grumbled, stabbing at her eggs viciously with her fork. "He has no right to speak to you like that, much less bring up . . ." She trailed off. All three of them looked up at her, then away.

Atria and Katia came from common families in Maniel, just like Lycas. They would have had no idea about her betrothal to the High Prince. The fact that Lycas knew about it was befuddling enough. And judging by the way they shifted uncomfortably, they were still unsure how to ask her about it.

Lucia's sharp, golden eyes darted up to meet hers. They shared a pointed look.

"It's alright," Val said finally. Katia and Atria's heads jerked up to look at her and Val's heart gave an anxious squeeze. "You can ask me about it, you know."

The two girls stared at her, as if struck dumb. Lucia, however, quietly turned back to eating her breakfast.

"I . . ." Katia began, her topaz eyes wide. "I didn't want to ask just in case . . . in case . . ." The small girl's face crumpled. "Oh Captain, was it terrible?"

"It couldn't have been easy," Atria chimed in, her hands wringing together anxiously. "Being betrothed to someone so . . ."

Bloodthirsty. Vicious. Heartless. Val knew all the words used to describe the prince of the Ember Throne. They were often the same words people used to describe the High King . . . and her own brothers. But as she looked at the two girls in front of her, both leaning towards her with understanding and sympathy on their faces, Val's tension eased. Her shoulders relaxed.

"No, it definitely wasn't," she said. "But you two were fortunate to be spared the ways of the Ember Court. Arranged marriages for the sake of power were to be expected for the nobility." Beside her Lucia's grip tightened on the fork she held in her long, delicate fingers, as if remembering her own past.

The Ember Court was ruled by fire and blood. The noble families were shuffled like pawns, all vying for the prize—power. Val's family was offered that chance, and she had squandered it.

Looking down at the table, Val swallowed the burn in her throat.

A small, freckled hand shot forward and grabbed hers. She jumped, just as a second, more delicate pair of fingers grasped her other. Both Katia and Atria stared up at her with steely looks of solidarity, clutching her hand tight in theirs. And in that moment, Val felt silly for ever thinking she needed to hide anything from her sisters. Suddenly, the memory of her hand on the general's leg and his shocked face flashed through her mind like a bolt of lightning and Val hastily shoved it aside. Of course, she could never tell them about *that*.

After breakfast, Val and her group headed off to training, her cohorts dragging their feet along, grumbling in exhaustion, and all the while, Val's mind spun. The whispers from the other soldiers followed her as she passed, even catching a glare from Elric on her way to the ring, and still, all she could think about was Aris and the look on his face when she had made a move on him.

She knew it had been a bluff—Aris probably knew it too—and yet, why did the very thought make her flush with embarrassment? As if he had truly rebuffed her.

Val threw herself into that day's hand-to-hand training with Lucia, hoping that the mix of fire and fists would shake her from her obsession with what had almost happened in Aris's office. Lucia was the only one who could match her in terms of power, so they were in a ring to themselves, flames rippling around them, dirt and twigs crunching underfoot. She sparred Lucia with all of her might, losing herself fully in the heat of her flames. Her Ember Magic was raging, billowing out of her in waves of nerves and frustration.

"Easy," Lucia hissed at her as her flames nearly incinerated a nearby bench. "Why so angry today, Captain?"

"I'm not angry," Val replied, but it came out more truculent than anything.

Lucia's eyes glinted. "Then you're doing a very good impression of it."

Val was exhaling great, angry clouds of steam with each breath. Panting and determined, her golden-brown hands twined firmly with wrappings, she circled her second in command, attempting to keep her core fire cool and under control. It was not easy, though. Each time she attempted to calm the flame raging inside her, the feel of Aris's thigh under her hands slunk, unbidden, back into her mind.

"Where have you been sneaking off to at night, Captain?" Lucia asked. She spun like an acrobat, a wave of fire reaching towards Val, who bent backwards, the flames barely missing the tip of her nose.

"Nowhere for you to be concerned with," Val panted through gritted teeth.

Lucia smirked. "How intriguing."

She leapt for Val, fists flying, flames curling her knuckles. Val's sore arms rose to block each blow, Lucia's hits coming heavy and quick with a masterful precision. She was pummeled from all sides, forced into defense, until, with a furious yell, a fan of white-hot flames sent Lucia flying backwards.

It was an out-of-control wave of heat—the signature Augusta move—something her family had arrogantly coined Heavenly Fire. The wall of flames did not wane though, even when she attempted to pull it back. The white tendrils raged out of control, wrapping around the ring, twisting in the wind.

Lucia huffed, hair smoking slightly as she pulled herself up from the ground. "Was that really necessary?" she asked, despondently holding up a limp piece of singed hair. "It had barely recovered from our last battle."

Val was panting and sweating profusely, swaying where she stood. Ember Magic to that degree raised her internal temperature to an intolerable level. Heavenly Fire never failed to sap her strength and overheat her significantly—a fact that used to enrage her older brothers. The memory of her eldest brother Lorenzo's disgusted curl of his lip at her collapsing within a ring of white flames sparked in her mind, and with that, the billowing flames flickered, and died.

Frustrated, Val ripped the wrappings from around her hands, feeling the scorched fabric crumble against her fingers. She stumbled towards the edge of the ring, flushed and dizzy, suddenly thankful that she was free of her usual armor that day. Even with her simplified outfit—a thin sleeveless top with light cotton breeches designed to let her body vent as much heat as possible—Val's vision still swam with white light as she staggered towards the water bench.

A warm hand seized her by the elbow, stopping her just short of toppling over.

"Come," Lucia said gently. "You need a cool bath."

"I'm fine."

"You're overheated, Captain," she insisted, tutting at her just like her mother used to. "Stop being stubborn." The sound made her smile.

Lucia helped support her back towards Light's Tower, her body protesting the whole way. It was a warm, breezy day within the mountains that enshrouded the rebel base. The sun shone down on them as they limped through the back courtyard, into the cool, shaded stone of the tower's interior halls. The minute the cool air washed over her aching body, Val let out a long, whimpering sigh.

Lucia scoffed. "You overdid it," she admonished.

Val chuckled and shrugged. "Sometimes you just have to let it out."

It was only as she looked down to focus on putting one foot after another did she realize her clothing was burnt almost up to her ribcage. While cotton was breathable, it definitely wasn't fireproof. Not like she was. Steam was still undulating from her body as they shouldered open the door—and almost crashed, headfirst, into Aris.

"What happened?" he asked immediately, looking down at Val and Lucia's smoldering clothing and glistening bodies. Val belatedly realized how much of her skin was exposed and was thankful for how her elevated temperature disguised the blush that was blooming under his hazel-eyed scrutiny.

"Training, General," Lucia replied briskly. "Captain Augusta just overdid it a bit. We need to get her to a cold bath."

Aris reached out a hand. "Let me—"

But Lucia stopped him. "You cannot touch her, General. You do not have the same heat tolerance that we do."

"I can manage," Aris said, giving her a gentle smile. "Besides, there are some things I need to discuss with Valeria anyway."

Lucia glanced at Val, whose panic was probably evident in her eyes, and opened her mouth to protest when Aris cut in again.

"Lucia, as your general, please . . ."

Val's lieutenant stiffened. She could never disobey a direct order, much less one from the general. With an apologetic look at Val, she released her arm and handed her over to Aris.

"Thank you, Lucia," Aris said, inclining his head to her. "I'll take care of her."

Lucia nodded rigidly and turned to head back towards the training ring.

Val did not miss the slight wince that passed over Aris's face as he slung her arm over his shoulder and wrapped a hand around her exposed waist. She could have sworn she even heard a sizzling noise.

"Gods, Valeria," he hissed. "How is your body this . . ."

"Occupational hazard, General," Val said stiffly. They began to stumble towards the endless winding staircase that led to the residential wing. She wanted desperately to wrench herself from Aris's grip, but her legs were still trembling with the weight of standing, much less dragging herself up hundreds of flights of stairs. His fingers were splayed across her bare skin—which she knew was still probably as hot as newly forged steel—and his touch alone was making her skin shiver in a desperate, needy way.

They limped on in silence for a bit, Aris's face set, as if trying to ignore the pain from her scorching skin. Val glanced over at him when the smallest hiss of air escaped from his teeth. "You don't have to do this, you know."

"I know."

The stairs wound around and around as they staggered up one step after another.

Desperate to ignore the prickling of her skin and the weight of his body against hers, Val asked, "What is it that you wanted to talk to me about, General?"

Aris's brow was furrowed in concentration as his heavy boots hit each step with a resounding thud. Val could even see a light sheen of sweat building around his temples. "I got some unsettling intel this morning," he replied, his voice strained. "I wanted to discuss it with you. I was actually on my way to find you."

Val couldn't contain her surprise that Aris was still willing to associate with her after last night. She assumed he would avoid her like a plague today. Instead, he was pressed up against her, closer to her than he had ever been . . . and she was burning the shit out of him.

"What kind of unsettling intel?"

Aris grimaced. "We'll talk once we get you cooled down."

The walk to her room took an unbearably long time. It felt like an age that she was pressed into Aris's side, his hands cool on her hot skin. The scent of him—like sweet-smelling earth and pine—had her feeling dizzy all over again. And she hated every second of it.

Finally, they pushed their way into her bedroom—the small space where her clothes claimed every flat surface available. Val flushed at the state of it, but Aris chuckled, the deep reverberation so close to her it made her stomach tighten.

"I'd tell you to feel free to leave some clothes on my floor next time, but I don't think you have any more clothes left," he purred in her ear.

So, they were back to this. She had been sure he wouldn't flirt with her again after last night, but she supposed that this was just who Aris was. Or, at least, who he pretended to be.

"Shut up," she snapped, and he chuckled again as he helped her stagger to the bathing room.

"Are you going to stay and watch me undress, or will you be an actual gentleman for once and give me a moment?"

Aris's eyes glinted, the mischievous twinkle lighting up those hazel irises as they did a slow, lazy scan of her already partially exposed body. "I would not object to staying."

For one, horrible, ridiculous moment of insanity, Val considered it. She had attempted to call his bluff the other night, only to confirm her theory that his flirtatious, playful nature was all a front.

And he had rejected her.

The ache of her bruised ego egged her on at his suggestion, but Val's rationality beat the voice away. Would stripping in front of him prove anything? Would it lead to anything other than pure disaster? The answer was, probably not.

With a heated glare, Val kicked off her boots and jumped, fully clothed, into the bathing pool. A wave of cold water splashed Aris, and steam billowed out of the pool with a gentle *hiss* as her boiling body was submerged in the cool liquid—which turned warm almost instantly.

Val's body caved in as the cool water tempered her internal flame. She could feel it go out, replaced with nothing but smoke and ember. Sighing, she submerged herself nearly to her nose, opening her eyes to find a slightly damp Aris examining the hand that had been around her waist, which was now red and blistered.

"I'm sorry," she said.

Aris smirked, brushing at his wet clothes. "No, you're not."

"I wasn't talking about the water," she said, and pointed sheepishly to his burned hand.

"Ah." He held it up, as though admiring the blisters beginning to form, "I've had worse. Don't worry." Crouching in front of her at the edge of the pool, he sat down, his gold armor bulky and cumbersome as he attempted to get comfortable at the pool's edge. He plunged his injured hand into the water before almost instantly withdrawing it. "Gods, Valeria, was this supposed to be cold?"

"It was," she admitted, smiling at him. He laughed, flicking water off his blistered fingers.

"It is incredible," he said. Almost absentmindedly, he reached into the pool and picked up her hand, which had been floating at the surface of the water. He caressed it, his fingers cool and damp against her still warm skin.

"What is?" she breathed. She didn't know why she was letting him hold her hand like this, but each touch of his calloused fingers on her tanned skin provoked a familiar tightening sensation. But this time, it wasn't in her chest.

"How our magic changes our bodies to adapt to it." He flipped her hand over, tracing the delicate lines on her palm. "Your temperature should have been enough to kill a normal being. And yet . . ." He rotated her hand over again, this time running a rough finger down the delicate skin of the middle of her forearm, causing goosebumps to ripple down her skin. "You are still perfect," he murmured.

They sat like this for a moment, Aris stroking her arm with a casual finger, Val trying to control the unruly internal flame in her that was flickering out of control again, causing more steam to rise out of the pool.

"What did you want to talk to me about, General?" Val whispered, breaking him out of his reverie.

Aris stopped, as if realizing what he was doing, before slowly lowering her hand. "Our spies have informed me that Titus has set his sights on something more concerning than Bridah."

Val cocked her head. "What could possibly be more concerning than Bridah?"

Aris's hazel eyes flicked up to meet hers. "Mount Cinis."

The rebellious flame in her extinguished almost immediately. Suddenly, her body felt unbelievably cold.

"Titus is attempting . . ." The words couldn't seem to form. Her body was rigid, and she couldn't breathe past the weight of the terror sinking onto her chest.

Mount Cinis was located at the southernmost point of Maniel. An active volcano, the heat and lava surrounding the area was insurmountable to any—even the strongest Ember Magic wielders. But its biggest allure was the dragons. As the only place the creatures dwelt in all of Krigor, Mount Cinis had become an object of fascination for many Manielians. Particularly, those of strong Ember Magic.

"I need to know, Valeria," Aris implored, leaning closer to her, "I need to know what the test of Mount Cinis is. All I have heard is that it is the true test of a fire warrior. And that there is an extremely dangerous prize at the end."

"Yes," Val whispered. "That is true. To face down the strongest wall of flames on this earth and survive is the only way to win."

"Win what?"

She looked up at him, and she could see the fear in his eyes, the concern. Aris so rarely had an expression that wasn't flirty or passive, but she could see every line of worry on his beautiful face.

"A dragon," she whispered. "A dragon that will become your companion. To do with as you please."

Aris seemed to stop breathing.

"But it is impossible," she insisted, rising partially from the pool. "It has never been done. Many have tried, but all have perished. The fire and lava of Mount Cinis are too intense, even for the nobility." She rose out of the pool, her clothes clinging to her body, and reached out without thinking, pulling his chin back to face her. He seemed to be rapidly spiraling into horror. "Even for the High King," she told him.

Aris stared at her, her hand still firmly clenched on his face, their gazes locked. Fear and tension were thickening the air like the steam emanating from the pool around them, and Val held her breath as Aris's eyes left hers. They trailed down her face, all the way down her body. It was only then that she realized that her thin training clothes were plastered to her . . . and had become very, *very* see-through. Everything was on display, and the general's eyes swept down her body.

Every curve, every angle was visible, her nipples peaking under his scrutiny. She knew he saw it. His regal eyebrow arched slightly, and his gaze darkened, all thought of dragons and dangerous tests seeming to fly from his mind.

"You should probably go back under the water now, Valeria," Aris murmured, but the sound was different from his usual, calm baritone. It was feral. Almost a growl. Something she had never heard, even in all his insinuations, all of his flirtations and impositions. There was genuine desire in that noise.

Instantly, Val released his jaw and plunged back into the water, her face bright red, her heart hammering so loudly in her chest she was amazed little seismic ripples weren't emerging in the water.

Aris cleared his throat and got up hastily from the edge of the pool, straightening his armor, rearranging his sword . . . tactfully. Val's eyes lingered on this and he shifted, turning his back to her, his hands on his hips.

"What are the chances that Titus will succeed?" he asked.

"His grandfather had tried," she said, her heart still pounding in her chest. "He lived, but failed."

She saw Aris nod, although he still had his back to her. "Tonight," he said, his head turning to face her just slightly, a corner of his hazel eyes visible. "My office. We will discuss this more then."

We will discuss this more then . . . when you are fully clothed and covered.

He didn't need to say it. She could already guess why he was beating a hasty exit to the door. If it wasn't so confusing and mortifying, she would have probably found it funny that, when faced with all the things he said he wanted, the general of the Pillar Legion turned tail and ran from it.

Val was tiptoeing out of her bedroom to go to Aris's office that night, only to run headlong into Lucia, who was posted outside her door, gold eyes gleaming dangerously.

"For the love of the Mother!" Val gasped, clutching her chest in shock. "Lucia—"

"Good evening, Captain." The willowy female was leaning against the wall, arms crossed, her red hair gleaming in the light from the torches overhead.

"What are you doing out here?"

"I wanted to check on you," she replied tersely. "But I also wanted to see where you were sneaking off to again tonight."

Val's face flushed with color. "There is no *sneaking*."

"Then why are you waiting for the dead of night to squirrel out of your room again, Captain?"

Val gave Lucia a flinty-eyed glare. "I *am* your superior, Lucia. Surely you shouldn't be talking to your captain that way."

But Lucia was pushing off from the stone wall, prowling towards her, those golden eyes of hers serious. They were always serious, but now they looked particularly lethal.

"Superior or not, you are acting suspicious, Val." She narrowed her eyes. "You're going to see the general, aren't you?"

Val felt her face flush. But she couldn't deny it, couldn't lie. Not to Lucia.

Her silence seemed to answer her lieutenant's question, but she did not smile. Her beautiful face remained stoic, almost stern.

"I swear, Lucia, it is purely for work," Val placated her, hands outstretched, practically pleading. "We are gathering intel on something. It's top secret now or I would tell you—"

"People are beginning to talk, Val," Lucia said, her voice dropping to a whisper. "You have been spotted heading to his office at night. You know what people say about you, about him—"

"And I give it no credence, nor should you," Val hissed, her temper flaring up again. "You should know me better than that."

Lucia's face darkened. "I *do* know you better than that. Which is why I know that there is something in your heart for him. Something you are not admitting to yourself—"

And that's when Val lost her temper. Sparks flying, flames licking her wrists, twisting up her fingers, Val approached her second in command. Lucia took a half step back from her, the slender female hitting the stone wall again.

"There is nothing between Aris and me," Val bit out, embers crackling in her veins. "We are working on intel he has received from within Maniel. As your captain, I have every right to go where I please. Do not buy into such heinous lies about me, Lucia. I thought you were better than that."

Val hated pulling rank. Hated it with every fiber of her being. She and Lucia were more than captain and first lieutenant. Lucia was slightly older than her and treated her, often, like a big sister would their younger sister. They were friends. She had, however, always accepted Val and her strength, and often yielded without fuss.

This was one of those times.

However, Val did not miss the spark of hurt in those golden eyes as Lucia backed down. Shame welled inside of her at the sight. She did not know where her anger had come from other than the strong possibility that Lucia may have been right.

"I only bring this to you because I care for you," Lucia said. She looked up at her, her lip stiff, eyes blazing. "Captain or not, you are my family, Val."

The words hit Val directly in the heart and she felt herself wilt, that unruly, roaring flame in her core petering out.

"I know," Val said softly.

With a stiff nod, Lucia brushed past her, leaving Val standing in the hall, guilt threatening to drown her where she stood.

The walk to Aris's office felt long after that. Val's eyes darted back and forth down the empty, dark corridors, looking for any sign of inquisitive gazes. Lucia had said people had noticed her going to Aris's office, but all the doors were closed, the halls quiet and peaceful. The only movement was the flickering of the torchlight as she descended the winding staircase and crept down the hall to the familiar office she had been visiting for almost a week now.

When she pushed open the door, it was to find Aris sitting on his desk, flipping through an old, leather tome. He was in his usual state of casual dress, which he donned on nights like these. Devoid of his usual gold armor, the plain white tunic he wore hugged every inch of his body. It was opened at the collar, exposing his bronzed chest slightly in a way that made her throat dry.

He looked up as she entered. "Something delay you?"

"Lucia," she muttered. The memory of her second's face at her outburst made shame flood her insides again.

Aris tilted his head. "What did she want?"

"It's nothing." Val walked into the room, shutting the door firmly behind her. She was not going to tell Aris the whole Legion apparently suspected they were having an affair. She already knew they attributed her promotion to captain to the fact she must have bedded the general and he had felt obligated. The whispers had been even louder lately, more blatant. They actively laughed at her now. But she wouldn't burden Aris with that.

Val sat down in her usual seat, trying to reel in her anxiety. She had always thought of Light's Tower as more of a home than the Augusta Manor had ever been. Here, she had three people who cared for her unconditionally, like siblings.

Her real siblings had bullied and beaten her to within an inch of her life . . . Sometimes did even worse than that. Lucia, Katia, and Atria would kill for her. Would *die* for her. The thought of her three officers made her heart swell with love and gratitude, and yet the rest of Light's Tower did not seem to regard her with nearly as much respect.

Pressing a hand to her mouth, Val hid her face from the general, attempting to steady herself. The heaviness in her heart at that moment was so overwhelming it was hard for her to keep it in.

Aris immediately noticed this. Lowering the book, he slid off the table and sat in the chair beside her.

"What's wrong, Valeria?"

Did he see the tears glimmering in her eyes? Perhaps he saw her rage at the fact that she cared so deeply what the Legion thought of her. She had never cared what people thought of her, never cared how her family had rejected her, or how her brothers had resented her. Yet, she cared what this group of misfits felt. And if she were a misfit from the misfits, what was left for her?

"It's nothing," Val said again, rubbing at her eyes, hoping Aris didn't notice the moisture behind them.

"Valeria." His voice was stern, and he reached out and seized her wrist, pulling it away from her eyes, revealing the redness she knew was in them. "Stop being ridiculous. What happened?"

She did not speak for a long moment. The tears in her eyes made the flickering candles around his office blur and twinkle. Aris held firm to her wrist, stopping her from rubbing at them again, stopping her from beating them from her eyes.

"Do you think I will ever deserve to be a captain?"

Aris stared at her. "Don't be silly. I have told you before—"

"*You* may think that," she said brusquely. "But *they* do not."

His hand did not release her. Instead, he began to do the same thing he had done in the bath: tracing light patterns on her hand, casually, carelessly.

"You are the strongest fire wielder in the whole Legion," he said softly. "Even today, that amount of power would have killed someone like Lycas. It may have even killed Lucia. But you . . ."

"What does power have to do with it?" Val breathed. "Look at you, General. You came from a common family, have limited magic, and you—"

"Are fighting with the rest of them," Aris cut in. "I do not pretend to be anything more than what I am."

He rose from his seat, releasing her hand. The skin felt cold without his touch, empty. "You are right. I cannot do much magic."

From his bookcase, he removed a small vase containing a long-dried flower. Gently, Aris placed it on the desk in front of her. Holding out a hand, a shimmer of green light glowed from his palm. As if watching time accelerate, the flower began to grow, its color darkening, petals strengthening, until suddenly, a bright red poppy sat in the pot, as healthy and vibrant as if it had just been plucked.

"You see, I would make a great gardener," Aris said lightly, causing Val to snort in spite of herself. "But besides that, it is nothing that could lead an army."

"You do pretty well without it," Val muttered, and Aris chuckled in that same self-assured way she was used to. Except, this time, there was a softness to his eyes.

"I do alright."

"Why do you put yourself down, General?" Val asked, shifting to look up at him.

He leaned back against the desk, arms crossed, face unreadable. "Why do *you*, Valeria?"

Val scowled. "This isn't about me."

"It most definitely is about you."

"No," she said, standing up too, arms crossed, mirroring his defensive stance. "Now this is about you. You are a great general, Aris. Why do you not believe that?"

"And you are a great captain, Valeria," he said softly. "Why do *you* not believe that?"

They stood like that for a long moment, arms crossed, staring each other down, so close that Val wondered if he could feel the heat that was beginning to emanate from her.

There is something in your heart for him. Something you are not admitting to yourself.

Lucia's words echoed in her head, bouncing between her ears as she looked up into Aris's green and gold-flecked irises. She could not deny that her body reacted to him almost instinctively. That pesky internal flame seemed to roar to life every time he was near her.

Aris's eyes were darkened, hooded by the dim lighting. They were running greedily over her face, her body. His usual seductive smile was nowhere to be seen. It was all heat and electricity, tension and conflict. *This* was the Aris that hid under the shallow flirtations. *This* was what had been lurking there all along, what had been threatening to be unleashed earlier in the bathing pool.

It looked like he had to rip his eyes away from her, choosing to look at anything else, as if that would stifle the storm brewing in him.

Instead, he reached down and plucked the now revitalized poppy out of its pot. With the same burning intensity, he reached up towards her face, brushing against her cheek. His long fingers stroked her hair out of the way, tucking the stem behind her ear, before brushing the red strands back over it. He didn't release her, though. Those fingers kept touching her, stroking her, winding through glistening ruby strands, trailing down towards her neck, pulling her closer and closer . . .

"Are you going to run away again?" Val breathed.

Aris let out a low, tortured moan as his fingers wove into her hair, jerking her almost roughly against him.

"I really should."

His breath was hot on her mouth, his hands firm in her hair, pulling her head back in a vicious strain that almost made her whimper with longing.

She only had the ability to moan one word.

"Don't."

And then his mouth was crashing over hers and the flame inside Val exploded. His hands were no longer cool on her skin, but hot and persistent, just like his mouth, prying open her lips to brush his tongue against hers in an agonizing tangle of molten warmth. Val's hands gripped at his tunic, the thin fabric now a hindrance. She clawed at it, almost burning holes through it in order to touch some part of him—some tiny bit that wasn't hidden by any kind of armor.

Then his tunic was off, and suddenly Val was being spun around and thrust onto the desk. Aris broke their kiss momentarily, only for him to lunge impatiently for her own clothes, the look in his eyes feral and savage. Hungry.

This was Aris unmasked, unleashed. And she worried for a moment that he was going to eat her alive.

Shoving her legs open, he pushed himself between them, hands groping at the collar of her corseted top, revealing the tops of her breasts as he let out a terrifying snarl.

"Gods, you are delicious, Valeria," he growled, and then his mouth was on her breasts, and Val's head dropped back as she clutched at the large wooden desk for dear life.

It was almost too much. She needed him back on her mouth. Needed him in some way . . .

Seizing his head by the top of his short brown hair, she wrenched his lips back to hers and this kiss was fiercer, more passionate, more demanding than any she had ever received in her long, long life.

And then, suddenly, it was over.

As if someone had dumped a bowl of cold water on him, Aris retreated, eyes glazed. Val watched as those eyes went from unfocused, to confused, to something else as he looked up at her, his eyes wide. The look sent a cold chill down her spine . . . As if he were *terrified* of something.

"General—" she panted, but he shook his head violently, stumbling backwards.

"I shouldn't have done that," he panted, his voice strained.

Val sat there on the desk, legs still open, blouse still pulled down, staring at the panicked general. He paced the length of the office once, stooping to grab his tunic and hurriedly put it back on.

"General—" she tried again, but he cut her off with another shake of his head.

"You should go, Valeria," he said gruffly. And, without even a single glance back at her, he stormed from the room.

For one stupefying moment, Val just sat there, stunned. Her body was still humming, churning with flame and heat, the imprint of Aris's hands still causing parts of her to tingle. Numbly, she fixed her clothes and slid off the desk.

Feeling used and dirty, she left the room.

CHAPTER
4

Val did not see Aris for several days after that. His absence was beginning to make her crazy. She was too scared to go back to his office at night, so she was forced to go about her days reliving that kiss over and over again.

Lucia was also fairly cold to her, and it made Val's chest want to cave in. If there was anyone in the world she would have told about the moment she and Aris shared, it would have been Lucia. Lucia, with her impassive face and her—only slightly—judging eyes. Val knew she would judge her for it, but she also knew she would not fault her, either.

Chances were, she already suspected. Lucia was always sharp like that.

It wasn't until nearly a week later that Val caught sight of the general.

Val and Katia were heading to training early one morning, making their way down the residential wing. Katia was telling her about a new sword style she wanted to try, when a door at the end of the hall opened.

A small, petite priestess hurried out. Her hood was in her hand, her face flushed, her lips puffy and red. Katia tutted a little at this, but a warm feeling of dread was beginning to fill Val's stomach.

She knew whose room that was.

Almost like a magnet, Val's eyes snapped to the door and locked with Aris's. He was shirtless and scruffy, his eyes empty vessels of cool indifference. Katia spotted the general nearly at the same time Val did and stopped dead in her tracks.

Aris gave them a brief nod. "Ladies," he said brusquely, and his door snicked shut with a firm snap.

Val stood there for a moment, the floor feeling like it was retracting underneath her feet.

"Never the same female twice," Katia muttered under her breath, watching the tail of the priestess's robe swish out of sight down the stairs. This remark sent Val hurtling straight back to earth, her heart feeling like it had free fallen through the stone floor. "Still," Katia continued, completely unaware that Val was withering away internally beside her. "I do wonder what the general is like. You know . . . under *those* circumstances. Almost makes you want to ask one of them, doesn't it?"

The feel of Aris's hands on her body, his mouth on her lips and her breasts seemed to overwhelm her in that second. But then, the image of his expression drifted back to her.

For the briefest of moments, Val had seen pure, unbridled fear and panic on his face. What on earth had made him look at her like that? Was it the kiss? Or had he simply lost control of himself? It was true that she had never seen the general lose control. Not like that, not like how he did when he had her in front of him, supine and willing. And yet, Val's mind kept spinning his words over and over.

I shouldn't have done that.

So, he *had* lost control, had yielded to whatever he had felt for her. Her stomach clenched as she felt herself wonder if he truly *had* felt anything for her. If that priestess scuttling by her was any indication, she was beginning to doubt he did.

Yet the expression on his face haunted her as Val followed Katia down the stairs, her mind spinning with the question of what on earth had shaken the general so severely . . . And if it had meant anything to him at all.

Val trained that day feeling sick to her stomach. Her heart was not in it and her head was a jumbled mess. She could barely feel her own feet as she led her soldiers through the training, choosing not to join them that day for fear she would be too distracted and get pummeled into the ground. All the while, Lucia watched her with a sharp, quiet eye.

When training was over, Val retreated to her room, not even bothering to stop by the dining hall for dinner.

"Are you sure you're not hungry, Captain?" Atria asked, her brow furrowed with worry.

"I'm sure," Val told her with a grim smile to both Katia and Atria, who were hovering over her anxiously. "I'll see you both tomorrow."

She escaped to the darkened staircase, reveling in quiet solitude. Her mind was still humming along, her heart aching like a sore muscle. She hadn't been able to concentrate all day, hadn't been able to unsee the flushed cheeks and mussed hair of that priestess. The image made a flame of fury surge in her chest.

As she ascended the stairs, she heard footsteps from below. They were light and delicate, only given away by the echo across the cold stone walls. Val paused and listened as the slight taps of the approaching person rebounded off the small, rounded passage. A hint of poppies and smoke filled the air for a moment before Lucia appeared around the corner. Her gold eyes were bright, even in the darkness.

For a moment, they just looked at each other. A dozen unspoken words seemed to pass between them. And then, without a single noise, they began to climb the stairs together.

They reached Val's room, and silently, Lucia slipped in behind her as Val closed the door and leaned against it. Lucia crossed the room, her lithe, tall frame illuminated by the fire in the hearth, and perched on the edge of Val's unmade bed.

"So?"

Val bowed her head. "Something happened."

Lucia nodded but did not speak.

"He kissed me," she whispered.

"And did you kiss him back?"

Val nodded, suddenly feeling ashamed of herself. Her fingers dug into the grimy wood of the door behind her, too embarrassed to even look at her second in command.

But Lucia did not say anything. She did not chastise her for doing the very thing she had warned her not to do. Instead, the statuesque female sat on the bed and appraised her with a strange look on her beautiful, angular face. Sympathy.

"Do not treat yourself too harshly, Val," Lucia said softly. "Many have fallen for the general's charms. You will not be the last."

Val's heart gave an unpleasant lurch. How could she tell Lucia that that was precisely what she was afraid of? That the thing she longed for the most was quite possibly the most protected thing in all of Light's Tower: the general's heart.

The only comfort Val had was having Lucia back at her side to face the constant whispering and snide looks from the Light's Tower's residents. She had even caught Saros averting his eyes from her, and he had been the most neutral of the group.

Either way, Val had thick skin. She could handle the whispers. She could handle the sneers and the smirks that some of Lycas and Elric's lot shot her as she walked past. What she couldn't handle, however, was Aris's total dismissal of her after what had happened in his office.

She refused to visit him at night again, even though she knew that their time was limited. If Titus truly was looking to conquer Mount Cinis, then it was imperative they prepare—even if it was for the worst-case scenario.

But after that morning, when Val had spotted the priestess leaving his room, she did not catch sight of the general again for days. Until the night of the Harvest Festival.

Light's Tower often tried to honor the holidays of the kingdoms Praiton had banned, meaning they had parties and feasts quite often. Harvest Festival was a loose interpretation of the Ganiean celebration of Gaia.

Gaia was typically a female-celebrated festival intended to honor their participation in a successful harvest. Now, though, it had become a general excuse for a raucous feast—especially in the Legion headquarters. Not that the rebels needed one.

Val, however, was in no mood to party. She had barely been in a talking mood for the last week—much to the concern of her unit. Katia and Atria had been watching her worriedly for several days now. And as she stood in front of the small mirror over the fireplace in her room, listening to the sounds of the party drifting up towards her from the floors below, she found there was no place in the world she wanted to be less.

With a muttered curse, Val threw herself back into bed, tugging the covers up over her head. She didn't want to go downstairs. She didn't want to drink and pretend to be happy, didn't want to watch the other captains talk and laugh together in a group that she was never invited to join . . . And she especially did not want to see Aris with that stone mask back on his handsome face.

At the thought of Aris, Val drew the quilt further up over her head. Gods, she was being pathetic. She knew she had messed up. She knew kissing Aris was a big, *big* mistake—one that she would now be forced to live with. How was she supposed to face him and everyone else when she could still feel his hands on her body, even now?

A large bang echoed through the room as her door flew open, and Val jolted in alarm as the covers were peeled back from her face.

"Captain?" Katia peered down at her. Her honey colored eyes were wide with concern and a light sweeping of sparkly dust. Val groaned and attempted to burrow back under the covers, but Katia kept a firm grip on the sheet. "What's wrong? Are you ill? Why aren't you ready for the party?"

After a moment of wrestling with her, Val relinquished the sheet and rose into a sitting position, attempting to smooth down her unruly red hair. "I'm just not in the mood, that's all," she grumbled.

Katia pursed her lips, her head tilting as she assessed her. Katia was always up for a party if it meant being able to put aside her leather armor and wear something pretty. Even now, Val's first sergeant looked dazzling with her long auburn hair curled and flowing over her dainty shoulders.

"What is it, Captain?" she asked softly. She pulled back the covers and sat down on the edge of Val's bed, a faint line of concern wrinkling her delicate features. "You've been a little out of sorts lately. I've been worried about you."

Val huffed a stray piece of her own wild red hair from her face and gave her a grim smile. "I'm fine, Katia. Really. You know how I get when we don't have any battles to keep me occupied. I'm just a little restless, that's all."

Katia considered her for a moment, her brow furrowed as if she didn't believe her at all, before her face spread into a catlike smile. "Well, then you should be thrilled to join us downstairs for the party."

And before Val could protest, Katia wrenched her out of bed and threw her bodily into the stool in front of her dressing table.

"Katia, wait—" But Katia swatted her hand away and seized her comb sitting on the dresser before beginning to work the teeth through her tangled curls. Val winced as she yanked on her scalp, but Katia held her steady with a firm hand.

"You really don't have to do this," Val grumbled. After the first few rough tugs, Katia's movements became gentler as the comb glided through her smooth strands. "I was perfectly happy staying in and reading that book you gave me—"

Katia shot her a horrified look in the mirror. "You were going to stay in and read a romance book instead of going to celebrate Gaia with everyone?" Val flushed as Katia glared at her, her hands still combing through her hair. "Now, why do I feel like you're lying to me, Captain?"

Val grunted, which earned her another yank to her scalp, making her wince.

"Now tell me the truth," Katia said. "Why do you not want to go?"

"Are you serious?" At that moment, the door to Val's room banged open again, and Atria bounded in. Her short orange hair was twisted back in its usual stubby braided pigtails, but for once, she was not covered in soot and dirt from training. Like Katia, she had dressed up—had even cleaned her fingernails, by the looks of it. She stood in the doorway, her mouth open in outrage. "Val, you *have* to go tonight! Why aren't you going?"

Val did not respond, instead watching Katia's delicate fingers loop each of her thick curls into a more defined shape with her finger as Atria sat down on the bed. Both girls' eyes were fixed on her in the reflection of the mirror.

"They're all still talking about me," Val said finally. "Elric and Lycas. About how I'm a slutty, undeserving captain."

Katia blinked, and Val could tell she did not expect this as an answer. And while it wasn't completely the truth, it wasn't like she could tell them what had happened with the general. Just to say it out loud felt like proving all of the rumors right.

But as Val hung her head, it was Atria who exploded. *"Fuck them."*

Val jumped and turned to look at her, eyes wide, shocked at hearing the words thrown so vehemently from her sergeant's mouth.

Katia's hold on her shoulder tightened. Then, in a small voice, she whispered, "We think you're an amazing captain, Val. Atria's right. *Fuck* them."

For a moment, Val just looked at her two sergeants, words momentarily escaping her. And then she mustered a small smile.

"Yeah," she said softly. "Fuck them."

And even though she still could not tell them what really, truly weighed on her heart, her friends' love pushed her to finish getting ready. They trooped downstairs together, and Val quietly hoped that some of their good cheer would rub off on her. Part of her felt bad she did not confide in them as she did Lucia, but she knew Lucia would always understand. Regardless of their steadfast loyalty and friendship, she still worried whether Katia just wanted to know what the general looked like naked.

The minute they reached the great hall, the younger girls disappeared into the crowd to retrieve drinks, leaving Val at the table, nursing a large mug of ale.

The night passed in a steady rotation of ale mugs, which Val downed one after the other. Eventually, Atria and Katia had rushed into the crowd to join the merriment, leaving her alone at the table with a stone-faced Lucia, who sipped at her own mug with a dainty pinky extended.

After several hours and five mugs of ale, Val slammed down her sixth mug and sighed, the noise lost amidst the laughter, shouting, and music filling the dining hall. To be expected, the two younger girls who had cajoled her to the party were half sloshed most of the night, laughing and yelling with the rest of the rebels, blissfully ignorant to her rotten mood.

It made her almost smile, though. To see the two people she thought of as her younger sisters throw their cares away, for once unburdened by the fact that they were in the midst of a war, victims of exile. During these parties, they belonged. Even just for the night.

Lucia, however, sat primly on the bench beside Val, long legs crossed, delicate fingers clutching a mug of ale as she analyzed the festivities.

"You could fake it a little better," Lucia said to her from the side of her mouth.

Val huffed, swirling her own drink around in her cup. "They made me come," she said, jerking her head towards Katia and Atria. "So, forgive me if I'm not in the party mood." Her eyes traitorously strayed to the front of the hall where Aris was seated, surrounded by Saros and a few of the lower lieutenants. He appeared at ease, his face that usual infuriating mask of calm. The memory of that face darkened with lust and hunger drifted back to her mind.

Val ground her teeth before tipping her head back, throwing the rest of her drink down her throat. Lucia watched her.

Feeling suddenly thankful her second knew what had happened, Val didn't refrain from scowling as she watched Aris smile in that enigmatic way of his at something Saros said.

"You're staring."

"Am I . . ." Val did not care. She was just drunk enough she could at least *pretend* she didn't care that Aris hadn't looked at her in weeks. She could *pretend* she didn't miss her nights in his office with him. She could *pretend* that it wasn't driving her out of her fucking mind.

At that moment, Katia bounced towards them, her eyes alight with drink and a soldier from the Laenimorian unit mooning after her.

"I'm gonna go up to bed," she giggled, her hand reaching for the arm of the male next to her.

Val barely suppressed a burp as she saluted her first sergeant. Lucia, however, turned an evil eye on the Laenimorian male. He instantly recoiled from her.

"Are you sure?" Lucia asked stiffly, turning to look back at Katia. Her face didn't dim as she nodded happily down at her. Lucia cast one last warning glare at the male, before nodding, dismissing them both. Katia and the male giggled out of sight, and Val rolled her eyes as she reached for another mug of ale.

"Maybe you should go to bed, too," Lucia suggested. From out of the corner of her eye, Val noticed Aris and Saros rise from their seats, still talking amicably. Elric and Lycas immediately latched onto the general and his group, and she felt bile rise in her throat.

"Maybe after this drink," Val mumbled. The general and the other captains left the hall, still talking and laughing amongst each other, and Val's grip on her mug tightened as fire spread from her fingertips, cracking the wood in a shower of sparks.

"Captain," Lucia said, a hand touching her arm. Val jerked and went to drain her cup again but found it was already empty. Lucia shook her slightly, forcing her to look into those sharp, golden eyes—so like that of a dragon's. She looked sympathetic. "*Bed.*"

Val slammed her smoldering cup down and rose from her bench, feeling as if the floor was moving underneath her. The hall was shimmering in a blur of movement, blending into streams of color and light. She was as drunk as the rest of them.

Nodding to Lucia, she staggered as she swung her leg over the wooden bench. Lucia jumped, her hands springing up as if to catch her, but Val waved her off.

"M'fine," she mumbled, sounding absolutely *not* fine, which Lucia's eyes seemed to scream as Val stumbled from the dining hall.

The sound of laughter filled her ears as she placed one foot in front of the other, her footfalls echoing in her skull. The party hadn't died down in the slightest, but all the other captains and Aris had left the hall. She wondered bitterly where they could've gone, almost laughing at the fact that, once again, she was the only one seemingly not invited.

Her question as to where the captains and the general had disappeared to was answered with the abrupt sound of laughter coming from the antechamber down the hall. Val froze, her ears immediately pricking up, hearing the sniveling drawl of Lycas and the corresponding snigger of Elric from around the corner.

"Quite a pretty little thing, isn't she?" Lycas was saying.

Val edged around the corner until the group came into view. The captains of Light's Tower were leaning against the walls leading to the administrative offices, all still holding their mugs. Aris stood in the midst of them, that easy, handsome mask still attached to his face. The sight of it made her chest ache. She was so sick of seeing that expression.

"I hope more of the priestesses come join us," Lycas continued. The runt was doing a pathetic impersonation of a swaggering male, attempting to show off to the others surrounding him. "Healers, too. Choices are getting slim these days."

Val rolled her eyes in disgust as the other males laughed in agreement.

"It is especially hard to find a female that wasn't already sampled by our lovely General," Saros said, grinning at Aris, whose face did not change. "There's not a single female in this Tower that the General hasn't had."

Aris shrugged, that empty smirk still on his face. "Occupational hazard," he drawled, leaning against the stone wall behind him.

"There probably isn't a single one worth a shit left you haven't had, is there, General?" Lycas sneered. "Well, besides *Lady Valeria Augusta*, that is. Too bad you haven't tasted that, General. Lousy captain or not, her tits look damn good in a corset."

The males around him laughed even harder, and Val felt the color drain from her. She didn't expect him to answer, but as she watched that beautiful face twitch with an expression of unexpected annoyance, she suddenly felt a strong sense of foreboding.

Taking a swig from his cup, Aris's jaw stiffened, as, in a voice as cold as his glare, he said, "Who's to say I haven't?"

The males around him didn't seem to notice the general's irritation as they burst into laughter and jeering . . . And Val stood there, feeling her stomach melt through her feet. Her whole body began to rise in temperature, redness flooding her skin, her vision.

The males were still laughing, still probably slapping Aris on the back, when Val stepped out from around the corner.

All the air seemed to leave the room when they all caught sight of her. But she didn't look at any of them. She had eyes only for Aris, who looked up almost in slow motion. And this time, there was no covering the look of sheer horror that crossed his face.

"Valeria," he breathed. It was so quiet that no one around him heard. Only she knew the way her name looked on his lips.

Lycas, however, immediately began the abuse. "I see now what it takes to be captain here, eh *Lady Augusta*," he jeered, but no one laughed with him. All their eyes were trained on her. They all knew she could set them ablaze with a single look—one flick of her finger—but she didn't feel angry. She didn't feel anything at all.

Tears filled her eyes as she looked at the general. The male who had convinced her that she deserved to be captain, to pay no mind to the whispers and the rumors . . . only to find him perpetuating them himself.

Shaking her head, Val's lip curled in disgust. Her vision was obscured by tears, but she didn't care. Disgusted with Aris—disgusted with herself for even letting tears show in front of these assholes—she took off towards the residential wing, not looking back. Their laughter followed her up the stairs like a bad smell, and all around her, the walls shook and shimmered in the water lining her eyes.

She ran up the steps, her feet flying under her, feeling cold and numb and stupid all at once. Then, footsteps echoed after her. Quickening her pace, she prayed it was anyone else but the group she just left. She prayed to Calida and the Mother all at once for it to be Lucia or Atria. Someone, *anyone* other than—

"Valeria!"

No, no, no.

Anyone but him.

But Aris caught her around the wrist, whirling her around to face him. And for the first time in weeks, Val looked upon the true face of the general. Panic filled his hazel eyes, fear . . . and something else. She wondered if it was regret, before immediately telling herself she didn't care.

"Let me go."

"Valeria, *please*—" But with a hiss of pain, he released her as her Ember Magic surged through her skin.

"You lied!" she snapped. Her voice trembled but she forced the hurt down, letting the surge of fire burn through her. "You told me to ignore the naysayers, but you *stood there* and *lied*—"

"It was a mistake, Valeria!" he pleaded, making to reach for her again but stopping himself short. "I didn't think about what I was saying. I just wanted them to shut up and I—"

"You were bragging." Val glared down at him, unable to stop that stupid quiver of her chin. "After everything I've told you . . . You stood there in front of a group who undermines me for being a female every chance they get. And you stood there and told them that we—"

"It was a *mistake*. I will set them straight, Valeria, *please.*"

But Val was done. It was one thing for her to be tossed aside after sharing something like they did that night in his office. It was another for the one person who had defended her against the vicious rumors to throw it all away by spreading them himself.

Val moved down a step, drawing closer to him. The panic in his eyes was still evident, even as she neared him. The heat coming from her body—from her anger and hurt—was radiating off her like the fire from the torch on the wall a few feet above them.

Aris's body stiffened, the general seeming to hold his breath as she came towards him until they were almost as close as they were that night.

She could still feel his lips, could still feel his hands touch her body. But, with a deep breath, she stomped all those memories down like extinguishing a flame.

"You will *never* taste me, General," she whispered to him. And then she turned tail and fled up the stairs, leaving him standing there, staring up at her.

CHAPTER 5

Light's Tower had always felt like Val's home. But in the days after Aris's betrayal, it started to feel like a battleground.

It didn't take long for Val's unit to hear about the incident. Aris's comment had seemed to reignite the rumor mill that Val had not earned her captain's rank in any way other than on her knees.

"Just ignore them," Atria whispered, her hand clasped tightly around Val's arm as they headed to training one morning. A few soldiers Val recognized from Lycas's unit made kissing noises at her, laughing uproariously as she passed. But every jeer, every laugh, was starting to chip away at Val's very soul.

She didn't want to go to training anymore. She barely wanted to leave her room. But every morning, Lucia was at her door, waiting for her.

"You do not hide from these people," Lucia told her.

But that was all she wanted to do. Hide.

Until the day that Aris burst through her bedroom door.

"What in the *Mother*—" Val sprang from her bed. She had been lying down, pouring over some fluffy book Katia had given her, but it went flying with the crash of her door against the wall.

Aris was panting, his face white. He was wearing his usual tunic that clung to him in all the right—and *very* wrong—places. She never thought she would miss the armor so much.

"General, I'm really not in the mood," she snapped, but the sheer panic on his face as he shook his head made Val forget for a second how angry she was at him.

"T-Titus," he panted.

Val stilled. "What about him?" But she knew the answer. One look at Aris's face told her all she needed to know. Nothing else would panic the general like this. Nothing else besides maybe kissing her like the world was ending.

"He did it . . .?" she whispered.

The general stumbled into her room, pushing the door closed and slumping against it, his face ashen. He was in such a state that Val didn't even have time to be worried about being alone in a room with him again for the first time in weeks.

"I just got word from our spies in Maniel," he told her. "They said Titus flew over the Red Citadel on the back of an enormous, winged beast."

Val's heart skipped a beat. Titus had always been a terrifying, bloodthirsty brute. She had only met the male once or twice, the last being when she was young—barely out of adolescence. There was nothing that terrified her more than seeing him in the throne room of the Red Citadel. How his gaze had swept her body, those red eyes of his gleaming when he told her parents that she had "blossomed nicely." How she would make a valuable bride for his son . . .

To picture the High King on the back of a deadly, winged beast—one that could burn whole kingdoms to the ground—she did not want to think . . .

Aris slumped down on the edge of her bed, rubbing his face with a rough hand. The mattress sank with his weight, and Val felt herself instinctively draw her legs to her chest. It was only then that she realized she was in her very thin, very short nightgown. Gods only knew what Aris could see through the sheer fabric.

But Aris was not looking at her. His back was to her as he stared into the corner of the room as if he didn't see a thing.

"I'm sorry, Valeria," he whispered finally.

Val did not know what he was apologizing for. Was it for not acting in time to stop Titus? Was it for the rumor she had caught him spreading? Or was it for the kiss that both of them seemed to wish had never happened?

It was only as he turned back to look at her could she see the ghost in those starburst eyes. The hollowness that he always disguised. The empty cracks in his soul he couldn't seem to hide from her. She fought the urge to reach for them, to scoop them up in her hands and piece him back together like a broken vase. He was not hers to fix.

She decided then that none of it mattered. If Titus had a dragon, they were all as good as dead, anyway. They had more important things to worry about now.

"If Titus has tamed a dragon, time is of the essence," she said. It hurt her to ignore him, to not hear the apology he may have been about to give her. It didn't matter what he was sorry for. She would not let herself care. "All we can do is focus on what our next move will be. It is your call, General."

Aris stared at her as if he didn't know what to say. Whether he noticed the stiffness in her shoulders or the formality of her tone, he seemed to regiment himself again. With the swiftness of a cloud passing in front of the moon, the general composed himself.

"We need to warn Bridah . . . They must come up with a solution that could guard against even a dragon. I will call a meeting first thing in the morning and brief the Legion," Aris said, speaking to the fire, as if lost in his own thoughts. "We'll dispatch several units to the Manielian-Bridanian border as a safeguard in the meantime."

"I'll go." Val heard herself volunteer without a second thought. Aris looked surprised.

"Are you sure?"

Val nodded. She wanted to get away from Light's Tower. She wanted to do *something* other than pine and lament over the Pillar Legion's general. She wanted to fight and kill instead of sitting here, replaying how it felt to kiss him, how it felt when he licked her bare flesh . . .

Val's face heated at the thought, something that did not escape the general's notice. It was at that moment both of them seemed to realize how close they were—and just how *small* Val's bed was. Even with her knees to her chest, Aris's hard, muscular back was barely a breath away from her. Gods, she could still see every ripple of muscle in her mind's eye when she had ripped his tunic off that night. Suddenly the room began to feel very warm.

She could tell Aris was remembering that night, too. The way his eyes swept over her bare legs, how his expression darkened, a shadow of the same feral look passing across his face.

For a second, it was like they were right back to that night, with Val laid out on his desk with her legs open for him . . . before Aris cleared his throat and looked away.

"I should go," he said gruffly. "There's a lot to be done, and if you're going to the border tomorrow, you'll need your sleep."

The knot in Val's chest tightened. It was as if her skin had turned into a live flame, prickling with his proximity. Gods, why was she so drawn to him? A moth to a flame, a dragon to a fire . . . She wanted him *right now*. Regardless of everything he had said, of everything he had done, she sat next to him on that bed and *missed* him. She wanted him more than anything in her entire life.

Which was exactly why she nodded, dismissing him. And Aris stood and left the room as if he didn't feel the heat, too. As if it were all too easy.

Val's unit was packed. The ships were equipped with supplies, their swords sharpened, armor polished, and apprehension high. Yet, Val could not help feeling torn as she prepared to leave Light's Tower. However, she was grateful to not have to hear the sneers of Lycas or Elric and their lot, since only Saros's unit and the smaller squadrons from Maniel were slotted to join them

However, she could not help but crane her neck on the loading dock, looking for a flash of gold, like she always did.

"I haven't seen him," a voice to her left said. Lucia came to stand beside her, her tawny hair pulled into several braids down her back. She looked every bit the traditional Manielian warrior. Val, meanwhile, felt like an absolute sham.

"Who?" Val asked innocently, but Lucia saw right through her. Reaching out, she laid a gentle hand on Val's arm.

"We are beside you, Captain," she said. "The three of us have your back."

Val gave her a grim smile in return. "I know you do. And I have yours."

They loaded onto the ship, Val's heart heavy in her chest. That knot of anxiety had been getting tighter and tighter since the night before with Aris in her bedroom. And she was still stupid enough to keep looking for him.

She chose to stay on the deck as the rest got situated down below. This was a long journey, one they had taken many times. Sometimes, Val wished she had been stationed on the continent to avoid this day-long voyage. But part of her liked the sea. She leaned against the wooden banister of the ship as they pushed off from shore, the sea breeze rippling her hair, gulls chirping overhead.

Her eyes lingered on the shrinking shadow of Light's Tower. From this distance, it was a jagged spike embedded in the mountaintop, its stone turrets visible from here. In all the decades of life she had already lived, she had never felt more at home than she had in that tower.

The Augusta Manor, with its curling ivy and red rose gardens, had always been more hostile than any battlefield she had ever been on. She was more prepared on battlefields. Fearless. At home, however . . .

Her mind drifted like the waves underneath her. Drifted back to what it was like to live in that large manor house. Her father and mother were respected courtiers and rarely home. They mostly worked the Ember Courts, leaving the three children home, alone. Most wouldn't think twice about being home alone with their siblings, but to Val, it was akin to being hunted for sport.

As the middle brother, Leonidas, came into his powers, he often liked to test them on her. Leo was the picture of a vicious psychopath, loving pain, soaking up her screams and tears as he held her down . . . and sometimes did more than just burn her.

Val shifted against the cold wind, shivers crawling up her spine as she thought of her middle brother. Leo had been obsessed with power. Had been fascinated with the thought of powerful families inter-marrying to make the bloodline stronger. She knew it had been the cause of his obsession with her . . . tormenting her, trapping her . . . touching her.

Her eldest brother, Lorenzo, did nothing to stop him. Lorenzo had always been a mystery to her. Cold and brutal, often holding himself with the regality of a High King, he did not torture her like Leo did, but he did not have time for her either. He rarely had the time for things that did not make him stronger or advance his military ambitions.

She supposed Lorenzo's treatment of her was preferable to Leo's, but still. The very thought of her brothers made her head spin, made her want to empty out her stomach over the edge of the warship.

Leo's voice echoed in her mind, *"You like it hot, baby sister?"* Val's vision blurred and she closed her eyes, attempting to block out the memory of that voice, of the pain, fear, and shame that would accompany those words.

"Valeria?"

Val started, whirling around and nearly losing her balance. A firm hand caught her and steadied her.

"What are you doing here?" Val cried. Those hands did not leave her waist. If anything, they tightened around her, as if they were itching to pull her closer.

"A general goes where he is needed, Valeria," Aris said, giving her a small smile. It was not like his usual flirtations; it was something else. An olive branch. A bridge back to how they were before that kiss. Before she had admitted to herself that maybe, just maybe, Lucia had been right. That there *was* something in her heart for the general.

Aris released her, and Val had to grip the railing again to keep herself steady. Strong. She had to keep things in perspective. Had she really so easily forgiven Aris for that moment during the festival? The answer was a resounding *no*.

"You are not needed, General," Val said coolly, turning back towards the sea, determined not to look at those hazel eyes. "I have everything well in hand."

Aris chuckled. "Lucky everything," he murmured.

Val glared at him, and Aris laughed. When she did not so much as crack a smile, his own grin faded. They stood silently, side by side, staring out at the waters, watching Light's Tower and the shores of Elbania fade into the distance.

She wondered if she'd ever get used to standing next to this male. If it would ever stop feeling like swimming in a lake when lightning strikes. The sides of her waist, which his hands had just released, were still screaming for his touch. She decided she hated her traitorous body more than she hated the general. Which was saying something.

"I set them straight, you know." Aris's words took her aback, and she shot him a confused glance. "About what I said that night on Gaia," he elaborated. He wasn't looking at her. Instead, he studied his clasped hands, free of gauntlets or gloves. Val could see every worn callous, every scar and scab that hours of hard training with his enormous longsword had yielded. But even though he didn't meet her gaze, she could sense his contrition. "I forbade them from mentioning it again. From harassing you about it."

Val scoffed. "As nice of a sentiment as that is, General, I do not believe they listened very well. You should work on insubordination in your ranks."

Aris gave her a crooked grin. She hated that grin. It was so dazzlingly handsome, so imperfectly perfect, that she wanted to reach out and touch it. Wanted to kiss it off his face . . . wanted to throw herself overboard just for thinking it.

"When we return to Light's Tower after this mess, I will see to it," he said. And then he reached out and put his hand down on top of hers. When she looked over at him, alarmed, it was only to see that hardened gaze of gold staring back at her. "I promise, Valeria," he said vehemently. "I will make this right."

Val stared at him for a second, before asking, "Why did you say it?"

He removed his hand, looking away. "It was stupid."

"That doesn't answer my question."

Aris sighed. "I know. I was just . . . I was just stupid, Valeria." After a pause, he mumbled, "Something I seem to be a lot when I'm around you."

They looked at each other, and she knew it was coming, and suddenly, she realized she was not ready for it.

"About that night . . . in my office—"

Val shook her head. "We do not have to talk about it, General," she said quickly, silencing anything further that he was going to say. "I get it. It was a momentary lapse of judgment."

"Valeria—"

"It's fine," Val insisted, turning to face him fully. They were so close, so alone. No one was on the deck, not a soul around but the gulls overhead and the fish under sea. But she could not give in to what she wanted. And she knew that neither could he. "It was stupid, right?"

Aris stared at her. His eyes scanned her face, before resting on her lips. The pull towards him was immense, but she pushed against it, pushed even when her own traitorous eyes lowered to his mouth.

"Stupid," he whispered.

"We won't talk about it again," she breathed, his mouth so close to hers that she could feel his breath on her cheeks. "It never happened."

Aris looked as if he wanted to argue. He wrenched his gaze from her lips and looked up at her with wide hazel eyes. But something seemed to harden in them. And then he took a step back from her and nodded.

CHAPTER
6

When Val headed below deck, it was to find Lucia, Katia, and Atria waiting for her in her small captain's cabin. Most of the other soldiers had to sleep in steerage, with only one or two cabins available for those of the highest rank onboard. Val always made it a point to share her quarters with her unit. She regretted this, however, when all three of them looked up as she walked in. And all three of them could see something was wrong.

"What happened?" Atria asked. They were all seated on the floor around the single bunk in the room. There was barely any space to step around them, but Val managed. She collapsed on the floor, almost squashing Katia, who let out a little yelp of protest.

"Nothing," Val sighed, but her friends rolled their eyes.

Lucia lounged against the wooden wall of the bed frame and raised her patrician eyebrows at her. "Did you run into the general?"

The two other girls' heads whipped around to look at her.

"The general?" Atria cried.

"What about the general?" Katia squawked.

Val turned and glared at Lucia. "Thanks a lot."

Lucia smirked. But the damage was done. Both Katia and Atria would not let it go, and continued to hound Val, jumping on her from all angles.

"What about the general?"

"Did he do something?"

"Is this about what he said that night on Gaia?"

"Is it actually *true?*"

"For the love of the Mother, okay!" Val cried, waving her arms to silence the interrogation. The girls fell silent immediately. "Aris may not have been . . . *exactly* lying when he said that on Gaia," Val mumbled.

There was half a beat where it seemed as if Atria and Katia had been struck dumb. Unfortunately, it didn't last long.

"*What?*"

"You and the general?"

"No way!"

"Tell us *everything!*"

And at that moment, with her sisters clamoring over her, Val suddenly felt . . . normal. Like she wasn't a captain in a military during a bloody war who was caught in a torrid affair with their commanding general, but just another girl. Another girl who could tell her friends about her latest conquest and laugh and gossip. Another girl who would return home to her family after kissing the boy next door. Another girl who could hope for marriage and a future family. A girl whose life was not hers.

"It wasn't all that," Val said, blushing furiously. "It wasn't even *nearly* that. And I forbid you all from mentioning anything to *anyone!* Mother knows it's the last thing I need."

Katia and Atria exchanged looks between them, before glancing at Lucia. "Why does she know and we don't?"

Lucia shrugged. "I was in the right place at the right time," she replied.

They protested more until Val finally called for order again. "Now that's the end of that," Val insisted. And when they complained some more, she relented. "Fine. *Maybe* after we return home to Light's Tower after this mission. *Maybe* then I will tell you."

This seemed to satisfy them. Lying backwards on the floor the best they could, Atria rested her head on Katia's shoulder, Katia draped her legs across Val, and Val laid her head on Lucia's lap. They all fell silent, the crackle of the fire in the torch above peaceful with the slosh and slap of water underneath them.

"Tell us the truth, Val," Katia said after a moment. "Is the general really hot naked?"

Val kicked her and the small cabin erupted with giggles.

"I'm serious," Katia gasped through her laughter. "I always felt like he must be *huuuuuge*."

Atria gave a shriek of laughter, and Val couldn't help throwing her head back and laughing with her whole body. Even Lucia was laughing beside her.

"Well, if I ever find out I'll be sure to tell you," Val said, knowing she would do no such thing. Their laughter filled the cabin—Katia wheezing, Atria wiping tears from her eyes, and Val gasping to catch her breath. Eventually, they all fell silent again, their laughter petering out.

"Do you reckon we'll see a dragon?" Atria whispered into the silence.

"It's possible," Val whispered back.

Katia shivered. "I couldn't imagine the High King on a dragon. The only thing worse may be Lord Decius on a dragon. How could we stand a chance against a beast like that?"

Lucia tutted. "No more talk like that," she admonished, using the toe of her boot to nudge Katia. "We can conquer anything as long as the four of us are together."

The others murmured in agreement, and Val felt herself smile as she looked up at Lucia. Her golden eyes sparkled in the firelight as she smiled back.

Val had always thought that, between the two of them, Lucia was the better leader. She'd always hoped that one day, she'd be able to rally her unit like Lucia could. It was unfair to think that Val had gotten the title of captain over her purely because she was more powerful. Lucia was always the stronger leader. Full of grace and poise, she was everything Val was not.

But at least she was her best friend.

Without so much as another giggle, Val and her sisters fell asleep.

The trek from the port in Dritus to the Manielian border of Bridah was as long as expected. The only consolation was walking with her unit, and that Aris stayed away. She hated the fact that her heart had the nerve to be upset about this.

"Are we heading to Burningtide?" Atria asked, jogging to keep pace with Val.

Val shook her head. "The general wants us further north. He thinks if Maniel will invade, it won't be anywhere near the Legion's outpost."

Atria mumbled something that seemed like a reluctant agreement.

They walked for miles, the cold coming from the western glaciers in

Bridah making her teeth chatter as they marched ahead.

By the time Aris ordered them to halt, it was midafternoon. Val and the three units settled in an abandoned Manielian outpost several leagues north of Burningtide Sanctum. The fort was old and dusty. Crates and barrels were piled up in rotting corners, the inside of the stone fortress reeking of dead rats and stale alcohol.

Lucia's nose wrinkled. "How long are we to stay here?" she asked. Aris was already in the room, clearing the dwelling, his large gold sword drawn.

"Until Bridah reaches a solution to protect themselves against a dragon," he replied, his tone terse, business-like. Val watched him move from room to room, his sharp hazel eyes skimming right over her. "We need an enforced presence on this border. If we can stay quiet and out of sight, we may prove to be an unforeseen obstacle for them."

"And how long are you staying for, General?" Lucia asked, leaning coolly against the dirty brick wall. Val shot her a glare. By the tiny smirk on her lips, Lucia knew exactly what she was doing.

Satisfied with his thorough check of the building, Aris glanced up. His eyes locked with Val's for a split second before shifting over to Lucia.

"As long as necessary," he replied, before excusing himself and sweeping out of the room.

The minute he disappeared around the corner, Val turned to glare at her second in command.

"Subtle."

Lucia gave her a catlike smirk and her friends brushed past her.

Val, Aris, and Saros began immediately delegating posts and duties. Camps were made, and by the time everything was situated, the sun was high in the sky. Val left her unit in their positions by their own camp in the west side of the building to head outside to take the first watch.

The desert air was beginning to heat with the afternoon, and Val breathed in the dry, acrid breeze.

Home.

It had been years since she had been on Manielian soil. She had always been too scared; reluctant to accept reconnaissance missions or excursions to the kingdom. She had expected them to stay on the Bridanian side, but this . . . this was too close to home.

The morning sun twinkled off a glint of gold in the distance. It was the very tip of the Red Citadel. The home of the Peruro family.

"You okay, Captain?" Val turned to see Katia coming into view. She was holding a bundle of supplies, which she had been distributing throughout the Nodarian squadron's ranks.

"Fine," Val replied quickly. "Go back inside."

"But we're helping!" Atria appeared on Katia's other side, her arms filled with heavy jugs of water that shone with the ever-brightening sun.

"Not by much," Lucia remarked, appearing on her other side, holding a spare shield and a few swords.

Val's eyes scanned their ranks, a bead of sweat rolling down her temple. The Nodarian squadron were grouped, Saros at the helm, beginning to set up camp. Val's own squadron was organizing the supplies, settling down within the small fortress.

She ran her hand over the hilts of her dual swords and tried to steady her heart. They were posted up at the border of Maniel now, the desert heat falling over their small numbers like a blanket. Since they had entered Maniel, there was an unbearable flutter in her chest. The hair on the back of her neck was prickling with sweat and something else . . . as though something was coming.

Val spun around, her eyes sweeping the horizon, before turning to the skies.

"What is it?" Lucia whispered to her. The skies were scudded with clouds, covering the sun. This wasn't good. If they were taken by surprise from the air, there wouldn't even be a shadow to warn them of the impending danger. Val's eyes scanned every cloud, looking for a wing or a tail.

"Val—"

"I have to speak to Aris," Val said abruptly. Lucia's brow wrinkled in confusion, but Val didn't have time to explain. The prickle of her skin, the fear licking at her like a flame in her stomach. She couldn't explain it, but she knew she could not ignore it.

Pushing through the soldiers standing around, Val fought her way towards the glint of gold at the front of the pack, her heart pounding in her chest.

It was standard Manielian warfare. A hot day with low humidity, luring the enemy to their homefield. Val had sat in on enough Manielian military strategy meetings to know what a perfect day for an attack looked like to the elite units.

Val shoved through the Nodarian unit—Saros giving her an inquisitive look as she went—until she was stumbling out of the ranks, and right into the general's armored back.

"Valeria," Aris exclaimed, spinning around. "What is it? What's wrong?"

Val could only point at the sky, panting as she struggled to explain the sensation. How she just *knew* something was wrong . . . The capital city of Ignisis was only a few dozen leagues away, and even the very temperature had been increasing steadily over the last few hours.

Val babbled all of this to Aris, her hands gripping his arms as she attempted to get everything out.

"Slow down, Valeria, slow *down*," Aris said, his hands tightening on her wrists, his tone soothing. "I understand what you're saying, but I have spies within Maniel. If the Manielian army has an attack planned, I would have heard it—"

But Val was shaking her head. "This is not infantry," she whispered. "This is a special unit. And unless you have spies within that unit, you will not know this is coming."

Aris's face blanched. "What special unit?" he demanded. "Valeria, *what special unit?*"

Val couldn't breathe. The heat of the day pressed down on her, the thrum of the soldiers around her, the look on Aris's face . . . She could hear Lucia calling her name from somewhere behind her, but she felt like a hand was gripping her throat as she shook her head.

"*Valeria!*" Aris shook her desperately as he cried, "*Which unit?*"

"The Blood Riders," Val whispered.

All the color left the general's face. She could see his mind racing, see him adding it all up. Then, he whirled around.

"*Saros!*" he shouted.

The Nodarian captain turned. Val watched in slow motion as his violet eyes darted from Aris, and then towards the sky. His hands shot up and he let out a roar as he stopped a flaming projectile, just inches away from exploding right on top of the Pillar Legion.

CHAPTER 7

For a second, Val and Aris stared up at the large, flaming boulder hovering above their heads. And then everything went mad.

"*Shields!*" Aris yelled, and all the units on the ground simultaneously raised their shields. "*Squadron Four, positions!*"

The Nodarian units surrounded the boulder, and together, blasted the projectile off into the distance—mostly aided by Saros. But it was too late. Another flaming rock hurtled into the building where they had taken refuge, smashing into the old stone.

Flames burst from the impact. Val could hear screaming, see their soldiers fleeing the burning rubble. More projectiles were raining down on them, smoke and ash thick in the air as the units scattered, losing formation to avoid the fireballs crashing to earth.

"Get back to your unit!" Aris ordered and shoved her as a flaming rock hit the ground where they had just been standing.

Val hurdled to earth, chunks of burning dirt and rock hailing down on her. The heat was unbearable as more and more blazing projectiles fell. The Nodarian unit attempted to stop as many as they could, but none of them were as powerful as Saros alone.

Val sprinted through the ranks, watching as fiery hunks of rock crushed whole sectors of their units. Gasping, she stumbled and hit the desert floor, crawling across the scorched ground, choking for air through the smoke and flame. She didn't know where her unit was, couldn't make sense of any of the frantic bodies running around her, scattering like ants in a rainstorm.

They had been unarmed, unprepared. Readying themselves for rest, sorting supplies . . .

Flaming tar pounded the red desert ground around her, her heart beating like a war drum as the Manielian trebuchets fired. With each beat, her vision pulsed, the air moving in a hazy, fiery dream, the overwhelming noise from the battle washing over her, the heat suffocating . . .

Like it hot, baby sister?

Suddenly, a body tackled her to the ground as she attempted to rise again, jolting her out of her panicked daydream.

"Captain, *move!*" It was Lucia. Scorched and already bloody, her beautiful face was flushed as she shoved a burnt shield into Val's hands.

"Where are your swords?" she cried. "You have to fight! *They're coming.*"

"What?" Val asked, dazed, her vision still blurry.

"*The Blood Riders,*" Lucia cried, dragging her under the cover of a crumbling stone wall from the fortress that was now flaming ruins. "The High King's elite unit is coming. *Now!*"

As if someone had lifted the veil of panic from her mind, Val looked up. A wave of heat shimmered over the horizon like glistening fog.

Through the haze, Val could see nothing. Not the trebuchets, nor the soldiers. But Val knew she was right. They were here.

Val's whole body seized, frozen with terror.

"*Captain!*" Lucia's hands gripped her, jerking her violently around to face her. "*Look at me!*"

Val focused tremulous eyes on Lucia's sharp golden stare. She homed in on her lieutenant's freckles, the blood dripping from a fresh cut on the side of her angular nose. Something to ground her racing mind and out of control heart.

"I know you are panicking." Lucia had to practically shout over the sounds of fire and death around them. "I know who leads this unit, but we need our *captain*, Val. You are stronger than this. *Braver* than this. You are Captain Valeria Augusta! Do not ever let anyone make you feel like you're anything less!"

Lucia's words washed over her. Finally, Val felt her mind begin to clear. With surprisingly steady hands, she reached to her side and pulled out both of her swords. Flames shot up from the golden hilts, billowing out like twin infernos. Lucia smiled.

"There she is," she murmured.

"Where's Atria and Katia?" Val asked. Snapping back into her role, she suffocated her nerves as best she could. They were roaring to life, almost as if being fed by her anxiety.

I know who leads this unit.

The Blood Riders were the High King's own personal elite unit. They operated in stealth, the trebuchets being their favorite means of initiating attacks. They had been around for generations, each group more violent and terrifying than the last. But this particular unit was the worst of them all.

"They are gathering our unit," Lucia replied.

"Fall in," Val commanded, and they rose from their cover and sprinted into the fray.

Val's unit was hiding under shields. Katia and Atria were ahead, screaming commands, attempting to herd their numbers back together. The Nodarian unit were surrounding the crumbling ruin of the outpost, their eyes still trained on the sky. Val saw Saros, standing atop a pile of flaming rubble, his violet eyes glowing. She knew he was related to the late High King Castor, a distant cousin. This was their only blessing, their only hope to deal with the barrage.

"*All squads advance!*" Aris's shout echoed over the noise, and Val whirled to see the general, his gold sword out, attempting to hold control of the situation. He was scorched and dirty, his gold armor covered in soot. And he looked angrier than she had ever seen him. "We need to get out of range! Advance forward! Shields up!"

The squadrons who had managed to gather back together fell into line and began to charge forward towards the trebuchets.

Skittering to a stop, Val reached out and seized Lucia's arm as she watched the two squadrons advance into the smoke of the battle. "What are they doing?" Val gasped.

"We must get out of range, Captain," Lucia said, confusion as to why Val would even be questioning this evident in her voice. "The general knows that the closer we get to the trebuchets, the less of a threat they are."

But Val's thoughts were racing. All her years spent listening to her brothers plot and plan . . . All the memories of her childhood, sitting within war meetings and learning Manielian battle strategies were thundering in her mind.

"*Stop!*" Val shouted, throwing out an arm to hold back her unit from following the other squadrons. "Do not advance!" But it was too late. The other two squadrons had moved forward at Aris's command and were suddenly lit up in a volley of flames and swords.

Lucia cried out, lunging forward, but Val stopped her from running to their aid. The sounds of their soldiers' screams faded with the flickering flames, and then, through the smoke, a flash of red armor glinted in the desert sun.

They had been waiting for them to push up, knowing fully it was a game of cat and mouse. Knowing that, to get out of range, they had to advance.

Val felt a hand grip her heart, squeezing tightly. And then she saw red.

"It's no matter," Val growled, the flames exploding across her swords with her fury. "We see them now."

Lucia whipped around to look at her. "You intend to fight?"

Val only nodded. Oh, she intended to fight. The blood was boiling in her veins as she beheld the burnt bodies of three of the five squadrons they had traveled with. She did not care about her own safety anymore. She had just watched more than half of their comrades go up in flames. In that moment, she no longer feared the fire. In that moment, she became it.

And now she wanted blood.

"Ready positions!" Val shouted to her ranks. Val's unit was well-trained. Hand to hand combat was their specialty. A mix of Ember Magic and Water Magic users, they worked in tandem, compensating for each other's weaknesses.

At Val's order, they sprang to attention. Even Lucia, Atria, and Katia snapped to the ready, although their expressions were dubious.

"Valeria!" Aris shouted from his vantage point atop the crumbling base. "*What are you doing?* We must retreat!"

But Val did not hear him. All she could hear was her own blood pounding in her ears. And when she advanced towards the group of red armored soldiers, she did not hear the general screaming at her to stop.

The first strike came from the right flank. Val parried a spear with one sword, fire shooting out from her left, blasting an advancing soldier who was charging her way. Lucia exploded into the fray a second later, followed by Katia, then Atria. And then, Val's whole unit was locked in battle.

Val fought like a female possessed. The slash of her blades, the slicing of flesh from bone only fueled her. Fire was licking every inch of her body, the inferno building with flames both from Val's unit and their enemy, but none of it stopped her.

She could go further; the heat of their flames was nothing to her. She would not stop until they were all dead, she wouldn't rest until they were dust at her feet, she—

Arms encircled her neck, trapping her against blistering heat. A cool, hooked knife pressed against her throat, halting her deadly rampage. And then a voice breathed in her ear, "Look at how murderous you've become . . . baby sister."

The flame within her—which a second ago, had been roaring out of control—froze in her veins. A familiar gold hooked blade pressed against her throat, the screaming inferno of white-hot flames that suddenly erupted in a ring around her, blasting out everyone in her unit. Leaving only her . . . her and her older brother.

"Leo—" Val breathed. In the minute of silence between the flames and the battle, Val could hear voices screaming her name. And then she was face down in the sand, Leo on top of her.

"Leo, stop—!" Val was choking on the dust and smoke, but Leo was laughing too loud, drowning out her cries.

"What's wrong, baby sister?" he cackled in her ear. "Didn't you miss me?"

Val bucked her legs underneath him, desperately trying to get her face free of the dirt, but Leo's knee pressed harder into her back. She thrashed her feet, threw her elbows, and managed to jerk herself onto her back, finally coming face to face with her middle brother.

Short ruby red hair fell into his eyes, his mouth stretched into a ghoulish smile as he leered down at her. Tall, and wiry, Leo might have been handsome if it wasn't for the manic gleam in those familiar amber eyes. The murderous spark warped his features, making him look deranged.

Spitting her hair out of her mouth, Val turned her head to look around. A ring of Heavenly Fire had erupted around them, isolating her from anyone who could help. Through the flickering flames, Val could see Lucia, Atria, and Katia staring back at her. They were dirty, burnt and bleeding, as if they had tried and failed to make it through Leo's fire to rescue her . . . and were being held back from trying again by Aris. The general was staring through the flames, his handsome face scorched and bloody . . . and unmistakably horrified.

Suddenly, a streak of fire rocketed over their heads as a trebuchet released another projectile into the air. Val gasped, wrenching her gaze away from the general's face to watch as the flaming missile arced over them, and straight towards Bridah's walls. A loud explosion shook the canyon and Val screamed, bucking underneath Leo, trying desperately to break loose. But when Aris's shout mixed with Leo's horrible scream of mirth, Val knew.

Bridah's wall had been breached.

"Wanna watch us send Bridah up in flames?" Leo breathed in her ear, his hand clamping back down around her face, forcing her into the ground again. "Wanna listen to them scream, baby sister?"

Moving furiously, Val tore her face free from Leo's grasp just to stare through the flickering white flames, back towards the remainder of the Legion forces, which had begun to surge towards Bridah's wall. Val's heart lurched into her throat as she locked eyes with the general. His face was ghostly white as he watched her brother pin her to the ground, torn between going to her aid and rushing to Bridah's.

"*Aris!*" she screamed as Leo's knife dug into her neck. She gasped as the tip began to draw blood. "*Aris! Go! Get them out of here!*"

The general was holding Lucia around the middle as she fought, tooth and nail, screaming Val's name louder than even the roar of the flames. Katia was holding Atria, but there were wet tracks on her face where her tears had run through the soot.

"Now, now," Leo snarled, grabbing her by the face and jerking her back to him again. "It's just you and me right now. Leave your dirty rebel friends out of this. This is a family matter."

But she didn't care about any of it. All she cared about was Aris and her friends getting as far away from here as possible. The Blood Riders had already breached the wall. She had no idea how many of them were now entering the Frost Kingdom, nor how many of the Legion remained to stop them. And the general . . . the general seemed frozen as he watched her, holding back her three best friends as they screamed her name through a wall of fire.

"*Hold still,*" Leo hissed, and his hand slammed down on her throat, pinning her head to the ground. Val gasped for air, spluttering against the tightening golden fingers. "What do you and your little friends think you're doing here, *Vilaya?*" he whispered into her ear. "You think you can stop what we're doing?"

Val's skin crawled at the word . . . her name in Materín, Maniel's ancient mother tongue. Only her family had ever called her that.

"Why aren't you answering me?" Leo crowed, his hot breath caressing her face like a dragon's flame. "Have you still not learned to be obedient, baby sister? Perhaps I need to teach you a lesson again like I used to?" Flames unfurled from his fingers and the tender skin of Val's neck began to heat.

"No . . . Leo, stop, *please!*" But her words were lost in Leo's yell of glee as fire burst from the hand still fisted around her throat. A billowing inferno engulfed Val and her consequent scream of pain. Leo's flames were hot—hotter than what she could withstand . . . but only barely. Just enough to cause pain. He was toying with her. This was only a taste . . .

The flames died down and Val's screams abated, but she could now feel tears streaking her newly blistered skin. The warrior in her who had been fighting only minutes ago was gone, destroyed in an instant. Now, pinned beneath her older brother, she was nothing but a scared little girl again, sobbing and screaming for someone to help her who would never come.

"I forgot how delicious your screams are," Leo snarled, lowering his face into her neck, and breathing in. Val's skin crawled and she choked on more sobs.

Through her tears, she could still see her unit fighting to get to her . . . but her eyes were drawn to Aris again, who was watching in a petrified trance as Leo's tongue flicked out and ran along her neck.

Val reached out to hit him, to shove him off her, but his other hand holding the knife came down and plunged into her shoulder. She screamed but her body was trapped under his weight.

All around them, the remaining Legion soldiers fought the Blood Riders at the opening in Bridah's wall. The sounds of the battle echoed through the red desert, yet all the while, Aris remained, rooted to the spot, still clinging to Val's sisters, who were attempting to push past him, all of them still screaming her name.

She didn't understand why he still stood there . . . didn't understand why he wasn't going to the Legion's aid, taking her sisters with him—

Go, Aris, Val pleaded mentally, staring through her tears at the general holding her friends back. *Take them and go . . . please . . .*

She couldn't bear the thought of having them see this, having to see what her brother truly was. But, by the look on Aris's face, Val knew he had realized it. The horror was evident in those hazel eyes, and she wondered if they'd ever look at her the same again.

Leo's laugh was crazed, flickers of flame unfurling from the corners of his mouth. "I'm gonna make you bleed again, *Vilaya,*" he sang. "Unless you tell me what it is you filthy rebels think you're doing here. Perhaps you've come back to tell your dear brothers that you've made a mistake? That you're through disgracing the Augusta name . . ." His tongue grazed her burnt flesh again, and she fought back the heave of revulsion in her stomach. "We will take you back, little sister. Either as an ally or in pieces. It's your choice."

He pushed the knife deeper into her shoulder, and Val let out another scream. It was muffled by the hand still clamped around her throat, flames licking at her chin.

"I . . . won't . . ." The words sputtered from her. She couldn't seem to be able to string together a sentence. Her whole body was screaming in pain and fear.

"What was that?" Leo sang, leaning closer, his body weight sinking onto the hilt of the knife in her shoulder, and she felt it hit bone. "You'll have to speak up a little louder."

"I . . . will never . . . come back with you," Val spat, the pain in her shoulder and neck beginning to blind her. "I'd rather be burned alive than go home with you, *Leíonum.*"

The sound of his Materín name following her pronouncement made the maddening smile vanish from his face.

"Oh?" he breathed; his voice so soft it made a pit appear in her stomach. "I think that can be arranged." And then his fingers were tightening over her neck again, and just as the flames were beginning to explode out of him, a rumble sounded in the distance.

Leo stilled on top of her. Then his head turned and whipped around to look towards the Bridanian border. Val craned her neck around him just in time to see a shadow fall across the boundary. Then, without warning, the ground began to tremble.

Leo let out a shout, but did not relinquish her, even as large, jagged glaciers erupted across the Manielian border. The sound of ice breaking earth shook the entirety of the continent as the wall of impenetrable frost rose, higher than even the fjords. The ice rocketed into the air, sealing off the small hole created by the trebuchets, sending red armored soldiers flying in a blast of frost.

From her place on the ground, Val watched as the glaciers shot like glass fingers, reaching towards the sky, their points jagged, sharp, and insurmountably tall. Even in the oppressive heat generated by the Blood Riders, the glaciers did not so much as glisten in the warmth. They remained tall, steady, and impossibly deadly. High and sharp enough to dissuade even a dragon.

Val let out an incredulous laugh.

They did it . . . Bridah had found a solution.

From behind her, Aris swore in relief while Atria and Katia let out gasps of surprise. And Leo roared with fury and slammed Val back to the ground by her neck.

"Is that what you were here to do?" he screeched in her ear over Val's strangled yell of pain. His fingers gripped her neck so tightly stars popped in her vision. Her own hand came up, attempting to pry the fingers loose, but it was no use. *You think you stopped us?"* Leo screamed, and then his hand began to glow.

An explosion rent the air, engulfing them in a blaze of white-hot flames as Leo attempted to burn Val alive. No longer holding back, Leo's fire intensified, and Val screamed and screamed as her skin blistered, her vision fading. The knife was ripped out of her shoulder as Leo held it over his head, right above her heart.

"CAPTAIN!" Lucia's voice rang over the flames, but all Val could do was close her eyes. Her tears evaporated in the scorching heat, and she felt her heart breaking along with her body.

"You like it hot still, baby sister?" Leo roared, and, with a cackle, brought the knife plunging down . . . only to be stopped by a withered vine. It shot out of the desert ground, wrapping its dried green fingers around Leo's neck.

Leo let out a strangled cry as he was jerked backwards by the thick stem, the hooked dagger flying from his grip. The fire stopped, and Val let out a shuddering gasp as she sat up, turning to look back through the wall of flames.

Aris was standing in front of Lucia, his hand outstretched, fingertips glowing, and hazel eyes burning with a fury she had never seen before. The general had never used his magic in combat. She had never seen what he could do. Even now, the vine was weak, and it only took Leo a second to pry it loose. But it had bought her time.

Val sprang to her feet, lunging for Leo's dropped blade. Seizing its golden handle, Val pulled herself to her feet just as Leo turned around. Her brother lunged for her, but, even with her burnt and blistered skin, Val dodged it, ducking under his outstretched hand full of flames, and with a yell of rage, slashed the golden knife upwards towards her brother's face.

Leo screamed, a blood-curdling, agonizing scream as blood flew into the air, splattering the red desert earth, flecking her face. Staggering, Leo gripped his cheek, blood pouring from between his golden fingers as he slowly lifted his gaze to her. His eyes were twin, golden flames of rage and, as he dropped his hand, Val saw what she had done. The knife had slashed his face from the corner of his mouth nearly to his ear. Blood dripped from the gushing wound, dribbling down his chin.

And then he smiled.

The bloody gash elongated his grin. His tongue flicked out, tasting his own blood. His smile grew.

"Oh, what have we done," he murmured. And, before she could blink, Leo was on her.

He kicked out, sending her spinning, the small blade flying into the air. She cursed, whirling around, attempting to find her other blade, when a fist connected with the side of her head. Lights burst in her eyes as she hit the ground again, just for Leo to leap on her, pummeling her head with flaming fists. With each blow, she felt her ears ring, her bones crack, skull rattle.

Crack! She was a child again, hiding in the Augusta rose garden. Leo had just begun to master his Ember Magic and she had burns covering her arms and legs. Never on the face, though. He always said he wanted to keep her face pretty.

Crack! She was a teenager hiding in the dark of her bedroom, hoping that Leo wouldn't attempt to come in again that night. Stooping on the floor under her window, she could still smell the soft scent of the ember roses below.

Crack! She was standing in the courtyard, covered in sweat and tears, attempting to master Heavenly Fire. Leo jeered, and Lorenzo paced. *More,* Lorenzo would say. *You're weak. You do not have the Augusta stamina.*

The blows rained down on her as her life flashed through her mind, and she felt tears spill from her blackening eyes. Until, suddenly, Leo was yanked backwards, and a familiar voice spoke.

"Enough, Leíonum."

And everything was still.

Bruised, bleeding, and broken, Val looked up.

"Lorenzo," she breathed.

The eldest Augusta brother stood over her, Leo's collar fisted in his hand. Where Leo was lean and wiry, Lorenzo was regal and imposing. His shoulders were broader than she remembered, exacerbated by the red armor of the Blood Riders. Long ruby hair was bound back, not a single strand out of place as he gazed down at her with a cold, vacant stare.

"I'm disappointed, *Vílaya,*" Lorenzo said softly. "After all this time, you are still weak."

The flames of the Augusta Heavenly fire continued to rage around them. She did not know whether her friends remained watching or if they had retreated. The tears in her eyes flowed down her face as she bowed her head, feeling smaller than she had in years.

"Lorenzo . . . *please.*" It was pathetic to beg, but here she was. Groveling at her eldest brother's feet again. He was right . . . it was like no time had passed at all.

Lorenzo still had Leo cuffed by the collar like a rabid dog. He growled and jerked against his hold, blood still dripping down his face.

"Let me go, brother," he snarled. "She asked me to take her in pieces. I will shred her to bits, and we will feed her to Titus's dragon as an offering."

Val spat out a mouthful of blood, glaring up at her brother, but Lorenzo's face remained stone.

"You are acting like an animal, *Leíonum*. *Heel*, or I will have to incapacitate you. Besides . . ." His steely gaze locked onto hers, and she saw the slightest hint of disdain behind those cold amber eyes. "I have things to discuss with our little sister."

With a wince, Val attempted to sit up, but her bones ached, her shoulder dripping blood from the wound Leo had given her. "I have nothing to say to either of you," Val said, attempting to remain strong, but her voice wavered.

"Stop wasting your time, brother," Leo sneered. "She already told me she has no remorse for what she has done to the Augusta house. Just let me cut her to bits and—"

Before he could finish, Lorenzo whirled on his younger brother. With a flash, he extracted the heavy gold sword at his hip and brought the butt of it crashing into the smaller male's skull. With a cry, Leo was slammed to the ground, his hand flying to the large gash the blow had given him.

"*What did I say, Leíonum*," Lorenzo hissed, his voice still as even and cool as the steel of his blade. "*Heel*, or I shall run you through just to have my silence."

Val gaped, watching Leo spit and splutter with fury, blood completely masking his features now. But he obeyed and fell silent, slinking behind their elder brother with his tail between his legs. Lorenzo had always been the only one able to control Leo.

"Now," Lorenzo continued, his gaze turning back to hers. "I made a grave mistake allowing you to walk free, *Vílaya,*" Val opened her mouth but closed it again as he took a step towards her. He had not re-sheathed his sword.

"I allowed you to choose banishment, not to disgrace and smear the Augusta name further." The tip of his blade reached out and scraped against the scorched metal of her pauldrons as she held her breath. "A *captain* of the Pillar Legion," he sneered, his soft voice barely audible over the white flames still roaring around them. "You not only disgraced our name, but you *spit* upon my mercy." The sword dragged from her shoulder to her throat, and the point bit the skin above her jugular. Val stifled her scream to keep the blade still, to stop it going even further. "I will not make the same mistake again, *Vílaya.*"

"*Laurus,*" Val sobbed quietly, her brother's Materín name slipping from her mouth. "Please . . ."

Outside the ring of fire, Val could hear Saros commanding the retreat. The Legion was leaving . . . but why wasn't Aris taking her friends and going, too? As if reading her thoughts, Lorenzo's eyes flickered away from her, instead, turning to look at what she had prayed to the Mother was no longer there. But Aris, Lucia, Katia, and Atria still stood outside of the Heavenly Fire, watching, frozen with indecision on how to act, how to save her . . .

"Perhaps, your friends could change your mind," Lorenzo mused, that frightening voice of his low, unhurried.

Val started. "*What?* No—! Lorenzo, please, I will do anything you ask! I will go with you, but *please*, let them go!"

Lorenzo's face was a death mask as he turned and stared down the general of the Pillar Legion. Aris's arms were still spread protectively in front of Val's unit. And he stared right back.

"I'm sure you are aware, *Vilaya*, that Titus's steed is circling us," he said.

Val's eyes snapped upwards to the sky, but there was so much smoke, so many clouds, that she could not detect a thing. But still, the knot of worry tightened in her chest. The prickle of danger that had activated before the attack was still there, even with the Blood Riders stalled while their two leaders toyed with her like a monster playing with its food.

"While the ice barrier is an annoying interruption to our plans," Lorenzo continued, "one command from me and the beast can incinerate each and every one of your friends with ease." Crouching down, he came face to face with her, his high cheekbones as sharp as slate, and not a flicker of compassion in those amber eyes. "Would you like that?"

Val stared him down. Her chest was tight with unshed tears, her body bleeding and defeated. Yet she recognized her brother's game. They were negotiating. Lorenzo always negotiated.

"What do you want?" she said finally.

Enzo's mask did not slip an inch. "I need to rectify my mistake, little sister," he said. "I will not allow you to walk free again. You come with us now, and I will consider allowing your friends to leave here alive . . . for now."

Breathing hard, Val studied her elder brother, but knew it was no use. He was unfathomable, as inscrutable as fog on a dark night. Cold and ruthless, that was who Lord Lorenzo Augusta was.

"Why?" she asked. Her eyes flitted towards Aris. The leader of the Pillar Legion stood not even ten feet from them, and yet her brother—the commander of the Blood Riders—was letting him walk away? It did not make sense.

For the first time, Lorenzo's mouth twitched into a small smirk. "Take a look around you, *Vilaya*," he murmured, that voice a gentle lullaby of death, a whisper of a breeze on a battlefield. "Your troops are dead. Even the ones who attempted to retreat. Besides a few irritating survivors, your mission is an abject failure."

He leaned closer to her, his finger coming to rest on her chin so she could not look away, even as more tears cascaded down her face at his words. But this time, they were angry tears. She yearned to seize her brother by the throat, throttle the life out of him, like he stole hers. But she bit it down as he leaned closer to her, his touch hot on her jaw.

"This was a victory, my dear sister. I will demolish your silly Legion, cut the head off that general and give it to you in a box while you languish in Ironbalt for the rest of your days. I feel that is more worthy a punishment than simply letting Leo have his way with you."

Leo gave a low chuckle behind him, and Val's stomach twisted. His threat lingered in the air, but Val knew it was her only choice. If she had any hope of seeing her unit survive . . . if she had any hope of seeing *Aris* survive, she had to come quietly.

Without another word, Val nodded.

"*No!*"

The shout broke Lorenzo's trance on Val, and she turned towards the pitiful, agonizing sound. Lucia was straining against Aris's hold, pitching herself towards the flames, tears pouring from her golden eyes.

Val tried to give her a reassuring smile as Lorenzo pulled her to her feet, binding her hands securely with rope.

"*It's okay,*" Val said to her girls, all of whom were sobbing desperately, pushing hard against the general's back. She knew they couldn't hear her as Leo fisted her hair in his hands and pulled her along. But still, when her eyes found Lucia, Atria, and Katia, she mouthed the only words she had never said to anyone.

"*I love you.*"

All three girls were screaming her name, their voices breaking her into bits, crushing her heart and soul into powder. And as they led her away, Val took one last look at her friends. And her gaze collided with Aris's.

The general's handsome face was twisted in pain. He looked as if he were holding back a tsunami all alone. But as he looked at Val, she knew he understood. Knew that he was holding back her sisters, not because he was afraid to come after her, but because he *would* come after her, that for now, the safety of the three girls were more important to Val than her own life.

"*Take care of them for me,*" Val mouthed. She did not expect the general to understand, to hear her from that far away. But his hazel eyes hardened, and he nodded jerkily before raising his hand, a glow emanating from his fingertips again.

And as Val was dragged away by her brothers, she saw something breaking through the cracked desert sand. Illuminated by the roaring white flames, a bright red poppy bloomed.

ACKNOWLEDGEMENTS

First and foremost, I'd like to thank my boyfriend, Cody. At this point, I think every single one of my books will start out with thanking you.

God, I truly don't think I would've gotten this far without you, babe! Thank you for listening to me tell you every single plot point and back story, and always being open to listen to me talk out some of my plot and character problems. Thank you for taking out your notebook and sketching me out the final battle for this story, and always being the master strategist I want Aris to be. But most of all, thank you for always being there to support me. Launching into this business has been an emotional rollercoaster, and you strapped yourself in next to me and held my hand through the whole thing. My life is richer, fuller, and more beautiful with you. I am endlessly grateful to the universe for giving me the most supportive partner a girl could ask for.

To my sister, who this book is dedicated to, thank you for always supporting me, and being the (sometimes blunt) words of reason. For reading my books, collecting the wonky covers like they're Pokémon cards, policing my business expenses, and doing my taxes—you keep me going in more ways than you know. Your strength, resilience, and sense of self are forever an inspiration, and because of you, it was easy to write Val's love for her sisters, just as it was easy to imagine her pain at their loss. Thank you for always being the other half of my brain.

To my parents—both my mother and step-mother—for reading my books and being my biggest fans. For listening to me cry over reviews, plot issues, financial problems, and also my crippling doubt in myself. Thank you for believing in me enough for all of us.

To my dad, for supporting me in his special, crazy way. For wanting to shout his love and pride for my work from the rooftops, even if it makes want to throw up and cry sometimes (lol). Your love and support means the world. Thank you for always championing me in everything that I do.

Of course, to Baby V, who will always have a spot in my acknowledgements. This series would not exist if it wasn't for you! I struck the friendship lottery when I found you! Thank you for always reading and supporting my writing endeavors!

To my amazing group of beta readers and critique partners: Isabella, Carrie, Keeya, Lucy, Angie, Christin, Evelyn, Mary, and Laura. The love that you all heaped onto this novella—even in my times of extreme self-doubt—is the only reason I feel confident in giving it its wings and letting Val's story into the world. Thank you for your love for both Val and Aris, and of course for me. You guys are the reason I write.

To my cover designer, KD Ritchie at Story Wrappers, my God. Just look at these covers. You work magic every time and are an endless joy to work with! Thank you for blessing my stories with your art!

And finally, to my amazing editors, Noah Sky and Jennifer Murgia. Noah, for always picking up every nerdy reference I put down, slashing down my giant, clunky sentences with a fearless precision, and generally waving your magic wand over my manuscript every time. I always have such a blast working with you!

Jen, your endless support and encouragement always finds me when I need it most. Thank you for not only being an amazing editor, but a wonderful friend I'm grateful to have found on this journey!

And finally to you, my readers! Thank you for giving my debut book A CROWN OF STAR & ASH enough love to make this novella a reality. The love you've shown me and these characters have blown me away. Thank you, thank you, thank you for everything xx

The black stain of death soaked her fingertips.

Deya moved her hands underneath the table, studying the pall that covered all ten of her fingers from tip to cuticle. From afar, it appeared as though she had simply dipped her nails into an inkwell. But only she could see the slight iridescent glimmer when she tilted it to the light. Like a shimmer of a threat. A promise of demise.

"The closest attack happened just last week," Aris said to Caelum. The Pillar Legion general sat across from her at the mahogany table within the Nodarian council room. His long limbs draped over the chair arms, legs extended out over the black marble floors. "Praiton wiped out a small outpost we had just east of Nodaria."

Caelum's jaw clenched, his hands raking through his white hair. Beside him, a diminutive female with a tight dark bun pressed her already too-thin lips together. Her robes glistened with the shimmering stars of the uniform of the Nodarian Prime Minister as she shifted in her seat.

"Do we have a plan for retaliation?" Caelum asked, his voice short.

The female's purple eyes widened. "Retaliation?" Helene Sidra echoed, horror evident in her tone. "Nodaria has barely recovered from our collapse, in case you haven't remembered . . . my lord," she added, as if remembering herself.

Shaking the small vial of dark red nail varnish she had borrowed from Val, Deya glanced up from the streak of paint she had laid over the first fingernail just in time to see the familiar vein in Caelum's forehead flex.

"Yes, Minister, I remember," Caelum grit out, his tone just as caustic as Helene's. "Unlike you, I was actually there."

Helene's eyes narrowed at the new High King of Nodaria. Caelum's spine was rigid against the high-backed chair, his fingers wrapped tightly around the Shadow Sword he had taken from the Praiton general. The Prime Minister's gaze darted towards the black sword, and her mouth got even tighter.

Deya was not much of a fan of the sword, either. No matter how many times she saw it on his hip, she couldn't get the image of it skewering into him out of her mind.

Deya smoothed another line of paint and moved on to the next finger.

Caelum's near-death experience was barely a month ago, but already the Celestial Kingdom was getting back onto unsteady feet . . . Starting with the implementation of the Prime Minister of Reconstruction.

Caelum turned back to Aris, shutting out Helene completely. "If we do not retaliate, we will appear weak."

Saros gave a dry chuckle from across the table. "The Legion just succeeded in taking back Nodaria, Caelum," he said. "This is the strongest we've appeared in years."

To Saros's left, Val sat quietly. Her chin was in her hand, soft amber eyes trained out the window. The starry night sky of Nodaria was dazzling, even from their position within Atlas Keep. Deya's Manielian friend jiggled her leg underneath the table, her gaze unfocused.

"With all due respect, Your Majesty," Helene piped up, her small figure shaking with barely suppressed frustration. "Nodaria is still rebuilding. Our people were slaughtered. Those who survived have been in hiding for over fifty years. There is a scar on this kingdom which we must heal before—"

Caelum let out a derisive snort. "We do not have time to heal, Prime Minister," he spat. "This is war. There will be time for that nonsense after restoring the realm. Unless you have no problem watching High King Ulf crumble, like my father?"

Helene's face blanched. She let out a splutter of indignation.

"How . . . How dare—"

Aris cleared his throat, silencing the outburst Deya could see coming from ten leagues away.

"Excuse us, Prime Minister," he said, inclining his head to her. "I understand your reservations about having Nodaria being active within the war—"

Helene scoffed. "We have no business being at the center of this skirmish when we have just regained our way of life, General," she snapped. "Perhaps you and your cohorts would do best to take your business elsewhere."

With one final stroke, Deya finished her last nail. The blackness was now gone, replaced with a garish red that reminded her of blood. While it clashed with the paleness of her skin, Deya didn't care.

No one had seen the stain; no one could question what it was. No one could be scared of it. Of her.

Deya let out a small breath.

Aris bent his head diplomatically at Helene and glanced back at

Caelum. "Perhaps we should resume this conversation a little later." The general's voice was still as smooth as butter. Helene's distaste had not fazed him in the slightest. Forever cool and unflappable, the general of the Pillar Legion stood, his gold armor glinting in the candlelight. The rest of the table followed suit.

Helene gathered her thick robes in hand and swept from the room, her gaze lingering on Deya. Her eyes narrowed—a sharp stab of mistrust—before she was gone with a swish of her starry cloak.

"Rayner," Aris called over his shoulder. The Sea Fae, who had been sitting beside Deya with the same bored expression as hers, looked up from the small figurine he had been carving with a short dagger.

"General?"

"If you are ready, the ship is waiting for you," Aris told him. Rayner nodded and made to rise, but Deya reached out, her newly red fingers grasping his wrist.

"You're leaving?" she said, her grip tightening on his blue-gray skin.

Rayner smiled down at her. "I have some Legion business to attend to. But I'll be back."

"What Legion business?" Deya asked, but Rayner shook his head.

"Can't say, but don't worry. I'll be back to check on you all soon." His electric-blue eyes roamed over Deya's head to rest on the Manielian female, who now sat, alone, at the table. She had not looked away from the window, had not so much as glanced up as Saros and Aris left the room.

"Keep an eye on her, will you?" Rayner said to Deya softly.

Deya shot a worried glance back at her friend before giving Rayner a grim nod.

Val had been like this ever since they had reclaimed Nodaria. Deya hardly saw her these days. She appeared for the weekly council meetings before drifting back into the black hallways of Atlas Keep like a fiery ghost. No matter how many times Deya had tried to get her to talk, Val would only smile at her with a far-away look in her eyes and assure her that she was fine.

Rayner gave her hand a reassuring squeeze before shouldering his bow and quiver and hurrying out after Aris.

Caelum paused for the smallest fraction of a second on his way out of the room. His violet eyes fell on her, but their cold, hardened look did not change. Without a word, he turned and followed behind Rayner, passing the large portrait of his father, the late High King Castor, as he went.

It was like watching Castor's white-haired shadow pass by. During all the weeks sitting in the same chair at these council meetings, Deya had stared at Castor. She was always struck by how handsome he was . . . and just how much he looked like Caelum. Aside from the long, midnight-black hair, they could've been twins.

Brilliant purple eyes shone out of the frame as he sat on his throne, wearing a rich purple brocade jacket. Between the Star Scepter in his hand and the silver chain of a gray pendant around his neck, his regalness was unmatched. Whereas his son refused to even take off his worn leather armor.

Deya stood, the bottle of varnish still clutched in her fist, and moved towards her friend. She laid a gentle hand on Val's shoulder, making her jump.

"Oh! Deya . . ." Whipping around, Val took in the empty room and blinked. "Is the meeting over?"

"It just ended," Deya replied. She did not know what was troubling her poor friend. For weeks now, those amber eyes had seemed haunted. She found herself missing Val's spark, her familiar firecracker personality.

Now she seemed muted, subdued like everything else under the Nodarian night sky.

Deya held out the small bottle to her. "Thank you for the nail varnish," she said, beaming brightly, hoping it would snap her out of whatever trance she was in. "It was just what I was looking for."

"Oh." Val glanced at Deya's hands and gave her a small smile. "It looks great on you."

Deya held her breath as Val looked at her fingers. She hoped it wasn't only because her friend was too preoccupied that she didn't notice anything astray.

Val rose from her chair, stretching as she glanced out the window.

"Are you sure you're all right, Val?" Deya asked gently. As a healer, you would think her bedside manner would be good enough to get anyone to confide in her. But Val remained stubbornly impervious to her prodding.

Even now, Val turned and gave Deya a stiff smile. "Of course, why wouldn't I be?" Her pretty, golden face was inscrutable as she looked at Deya with vacant eyes.

The last few weeks had been bedlam within Nodaria. Emergency council meetings scrapped together with distantly related relatives of deceased former councilmen, the constant retaliations from Praiton against the Pillar Legion in response to their retaking the Celestial Throne.

Tensions were high—Caelum's especially. The realm was not yet used to a new High King on the Celestial Throne. And, quite frankly, neither was she.

Yet it was Val who seemed to have stalled in it all. And Deya could only watch as her friend spun her wheels in the chaos.

They walked out of the council chambers and into the vast, cavernous hallways of Atlas Keep's east wing. The rounded halls were made up of black marble, the stars embedded in the floors and ceilings giving everything a slight incandescent glow.

Life at Atlas Keep had taken some getting used to. Once the remnants of the battle had been cleared away and the large castle restored, Deya didn't know if she'd ever get used to the way glittering trails of shooting stars would rocket across the ceilings, or the ever-moving orrery that revolved over their heads as they crossed into the large antechamber leading to the great hall.

She was definitely having a hard time adjusting to the ever-present darkness. Nothing but moonlight for weeks and weeks had her feeling permanently discombobulated, her body constantly struggling to figure out what time of day it was. While the rest of the Nodarians seemed thrilled to have this essential aspect of their kingdom restored, Deya missed the sun more than she wanted to admit.

When they reached the end of the wing, Val waved a hand over her shoulder.

"Well, see you at dinner, Deya." Before Deya could even open her mouth to stop her, she hurried off.

"Val, wait—" Deya made to go after her, but Val had already disappeared around the bend of the corridor. Deya slowed to a stop, the words dying on her tongue. It hadn't been too long ago that she herself wore her grief like a shroud. To see it now on her friend made a lump rise in her throat.

Deya sighed, and, suddenly, a hand shot out from behind a large stone statue and seized her wrist. Deya yelped as she was yanked behind the statue, but was stifled by a set of familiar lips crashing into hers.

All the fight that had coursed through her veins at the fear of being attacked drained from her body. Her red-nailed hands wound themselves around the white-haired male who had grabbed her. A moan escaped her—something she couldn't seem to ever hold back when Caelum was kissing her—and she felt him smirk against her mouth.

"What took you so long?" he murmured, his lips brushing against hers with every word.

A molten warmth was spreading throughout her body, filling her veins, as his mouth moved to her jaw, grazing down the soft recess of her neck. "V-Val," she stuttered, her brain struggling to form a coherent thought.

Caelum hummed against her throat. Hands gripped her waist, and his hard body pushed her back against the stone wall of the statue's alcove they were encased behind.

"And who is this?" Deya asked breathily, jerking her chin up towards the statue of the fae male holding a spyglass sheltering them from sight. Caelum's hands squeezed parts of her that made her knees weak.

"Pyxis, the twelfth High King of Nodaria," Caelum mumbled, his teeth scraping the tip of her pointed ear. Deya stifled a whimper as she braced against the smooth stone of Pyxis's back in an effort to remain standing. "Now, why am I giving you a history lesson when the present is so much more interesting?"

Gods, she was pathetic. It had been weeks of this. Caelum pulling her into dark corners, kissing her when no one was looking, sneaking into her chambers at night when everyone was asleep. But during the day, he barely looked at her. And while it was true he had many responsibilities now as High King, and couldn't very well go about kissing her in front of the council, he could, at the very least, acknowledge her.

She didn't know what it was that made Caelum pull back from her in the days following that final battle. And while he had grown softer with her since that day she woke in Nodaria's infirmary, he only displayed it in private.

She felt like a dirty secret, something to be hidden and ashamed of. And she had to be stronger than this.

Deya pushed against Caelum's chest, desperate to separate his lips from her body. If he kept kissing her like this, she would never be able to resist.

"You could've done this earlier, you know," she said, her breathing still heavy.

Caelum raised an eyebrow. "You want an audience for the things I wish to do to you?"

Heat began to pool in her again. Gods, why did he have to look at her like that?

Caelum's white hair was disheveled, the single braid on the side of his head the only nod to his Bridanian heritage had doubled. Now, several loose, untied braids hung from the tied-back hair gathered at the crown of his head. He refused to dress the part of royalty, still stubbornly walking around in his black leather armor. A soldier instead of a king.

At that moment, his purple eyes were hooded and devouring her greedily, his hands already reaching to pull her back against him. But she sucked in a breath and held him steadily away from her.

"No," Deya said, locking her elbows so there was now a good foot of distance between them. "But you could have at least said hi."

His eyes narrowed. "I said hi."

"You did not."

He then did a doubletake, noticing her blood red fingertips pressed against his chest. He quirked an eyebrow. "What's this?"

"It's nothing," she said quickly. "Just wanted to try something new, that's all."

At that moment, the thought of what else she had felt in the days since the blackness on her fingers appeared scratched at the back of her mind.

She had to lie. She had to. No matter how much Caelum kissed her, protected her, and ravished her, she was still scared that he did not trust her. What would he think if he saw the shadows creeping up her fingers? Would he think she was evil? Would he abandon her as easily as those she once thought were friends? Even with all they had been through together, Deya could not shake these thoughts.

The memory of Praiton—her former life—flashed through her mind, and small wings of anxiety took flight in her chest.

"You know how it is when that old bat Sidra is there," Caelum said, leaning back, no longer trying to fight against her. He crossed his arms— his signature defensive stance. "She and the council are already fighting me at every turn. Do you really expect me to parade this around the Keep? What would they think of me then?"

Deya crossed her own arms, and they stared each other down. Her irritation at the word "this" to describe what was strongly beginning to feel like a relationship lit a spark of fury in her. Especially since Caelum never cared to define it.

"Perhaps that you have a heart?" Deya asked, her voice waspish.

Lately, every interaction between them crashed into a stalemate, both refusing to back down. While Caelum's previous hostility for her had long since boiled over into passion, she found his mulishness as irksome as ever.

Caelum glared at her. "I don't need them in my business."

But Deya scoffed and shook her head, making to push past him, but Caelum grabbed her arm again.

"Deya, come on." He whipped her back into him, and Deya breathed in his scent—a winter breeze through a forest—and she felt herself yield just a little. Pathetic.

"I don't understand you, Caelum," she whispered, trying hard not to look at him. If she did, her resolve would leave her. "You never want people to see the best side of you."

Her hands tightened on the fabric of his black tunic. She wanted to sink into his arms again, but dammit, she couldn't let this stand.

"Deya . . ." he murmured reaching out and cupping her cheek. She melted like wax against his touch and stumbled backwards into Pyxis's back. Caelum pressed into her, and his lips brushed hers again. "I don't need others to see the best in me. All I need is you."

ABOUT THE AUTHOR

Victoria mostly answers to Tori and has been writing books for most of her life. After specializing in Creative Writing throughout high school, she went on to study Communications, Journalism, and English Literature. . . and stopped writing completely during this time.

After a LONG break, she recently decided to delve into the world of Adult Fantasy with her debut novel A CROWN OF STAR & ASH.

She now resides in Florida and spends her day working her day job, reading, writing, playing the Sims 4, and being a mother to a rotten Snowshoe Siamese cat named Sebastian.

If you want to know more about when Tori's future books come out, be sure to sign up for her newsletter and stay up to date with all *Fate of Ashes* related updates!

Visit Victoria's Website!

https://www.victoriaktaylor.com/

Connect with me on Social Media!

https://www.instagram.com/victoriaktaylorbooks

https://www.tiktok.com/@victoriaktaylorbooks

www.ingramcontent.com/pod-product-compliance
Lightning Source LLC
Chambersburg PA
CBHW061546310726
48972CB00008B/2634